WHERE THE
TRUTH LIES

WHERE THE TRUTH LIES

Helen Hayes
and
Thomas Chastain

Thorndike Press • Thorndike, Maine

Library of Congress Cataloging in Publication Data:

Hayes, Helen, 1900–
  Where the truth lies / Helen Hayes and Thomas Chastain.
  p. cm.
  ISBN 0-89621-161-4 (lg. print: alk. paper)
  1. Large type books. I. Chastain, Thomas. II. Title.
[PS3558.A8298W5 1988b]   813'.52–dc19   88-10280
                                                    CIP

no pr, *89B13492*

Large Print edition available in North America by arrangement
with William Morrow & Company, Inc., New York.

Cover design by James B. Murray.

Grateful acknowledgment is made for permission to use the
following: "Night and Day," by Cole Porter. Copyright 1932 by
Warner Bros. Inc. (renewed). All rights reserved.
Used by permission.

WHERE THE
TRUTH LIES

1

The often-quoted Hollywood wit and raconteur, movie director Jack King, once remarked: "In this town life doesn't imitate art; life imitates artifice."

ODDS-MAKERS PICK "THE AMULET" TO SWEEP OSCAR RACE The morning line with Las Vegas odds-makers is 1-2 that Arthur G. Strickland's production "The Amulet" will cap major Academy Awards tomorrow night: Best Picture; Best Actress (Courtney Ware); Best Director (Jack King); Best Screenplay (James Edgell); Best Supporting Actress (Halcyon Harper); and Best Song ("The Amulet").
– *The Hollywood Reporter*

The oil portrait of Arthur G. Strickland, hanging above the mantel of the fieldstone fireplace, although recently painted, had the quaintly passé look of those Man of Distinction liquor ads that appeared in magazines and newspapers years back.

The portrait was a reasonable likeness. The face was shaped long and angular, with the head held high and turned slightly to right profile so the dark eyes stared off at some distant point in the room. The thick black eyebrows were subtly streaked with gray, and so was the black head of hair, where along the forehead the painter had artistically restored some of what was in reality missing in the receding hairline.

Just beneath the portrait its subject, Arthur G. Strickland himself, stood surrounded by the guests who filled the living room of his Bel Air mansion. Beyond the open French doors at the rear of the room, more guests stood about on the terrace, while others danced on the floor of the boarded-over swimming pool to the music of a seven-piece orchestra. Multicolored strobe lights illuminated the terrace and dance floor. Waiters in white jackets served drinks.

The air in the living room was hazy with the men's cigar smoke and scented with the ladies' perfume, the temperature uncomfortably warm although it was a cool spring night, the decibel level of voices high with the cross-conversations, snatches of which could be overheard wherever one moved in the room — mostly shop talk.

"So I say, 'Solly, don't try to con me about what's due my client. Before I was an agent, I was an accountant — remember? I *know* between a picture's gross and net there's more gelt buried than at Fort Knox.' "

"You see her last picture? Fat? She looked like a queen all right. A drag queen."

Arthur Strickland moved away from under the portrait toward the front door, where more guests were arriving.

"We're shooting on location, we're three weeks behind schedule, the script's still coming in page by page, and the studio calls. Branner asks, 'Joe, you see a light at the end of the tunnel?' 'Paul,' I tell him, 'I don't see a tunnel at the end of the tunnel.' "

"We're all in the screening room. We've just seen the final cut for the first time, and you know what he says, actually says? He actually says, 'I think we all agree we'd have shot it completely differently, looking at things hind-sightwise.' "

Strickland moved more quickly toward the

door when he saw Halcyon Harper come in.

Jack King stood alone, a drink of Chivas Regal in one hand, a smoking cigar between the fingers of his other hand, watching the scene in the room. Sometimes referred to in the industry as "a director's director" (upon hearing the phrase applied to him, his comment had been: "Meaning certain directors watch my pictures so they can rip off my best effects"), King was of medium height and stocky. His hair was gray and crew-cut, his face more seasoned — in the sense of made fit by experience — than aged, from years of hard living.

Eavesdropping on the conversations in the room — easy to do with every speaker trying to top the others — he reflected that whatever else movie people were, most of them were bright and witty.

He figured that in the thirty years he'd worked in films he must have attended five hundred similar parties. More, probably. The thing was, with his director's eye, he half believed he could have told you what each person in the room was — actor, actress, producer, writer, cameraman, agent, "civilian" wife or husband of one or the other — even if he'd never seen them before. Long ago he'd theorized that in films it wasn't just the actors who were typecast; the very nature of making motion pictures demanded typecasting of almost everyone involved in the process.

Nor, in his opinion, had things changed all that much over the years, despite the big studios going down the drain, the big names becoming has-beens, the audiences lost to television, the soaring costs of production. The Hollywood of making pictures, for theaters, for TV, and, soon to come, for videocassettes, was still Hollywood, and so were the *types* of people who worked there. To put his own spin on the old cliché, the more things change, the more they remain more of the same.

He looked over to where Strickland and Halcyon Harper stood at the door, producer and star.

Arthur G. Strickland. There it was again, King thought. Strickland was one of the so-called new breed of producers in Hollywood: ex-agent, former talent packager, and now one of the most successful independent producers in the industry. And, in King's opinion, not that much different from the producers who had preceded him in Hollywood. Strickland understood a basic truth: Money and power translated into the muscle to get people to do what you wanted them to do. Which was how

— since the process was frequently a contest of wills among producer, director, actors, writer, sometimes technicians — motion pictures got made. Louis B. Mayer knew that, and so did Sam Goldwyn and Harry Cohn and Jerry Wald. Arthur Strickland was cast in their mold.

Then there was Halcyon Harper, star, who had just gotten into town from New York. Here, King had to concede, was not a case in point. Halcie, as she liked her friends to call her, was an original: star of stage, screen, and sometimes television, for five or more decades, winner of a Tony, an Oscar, an Emmy, a Grammy, and nominated for a second Oscar, and who had a Broadway theater named after her. She and King were old friends.

King set his glass down as Strickland led Halcie over, saying, "Jack, here she is, tomorrow night's winner of the Best Supporting Actress Oscar."

"I knew that when the last reel of *The Amulet* went into the can," King said. He kissed Halcie on both cheeks.

"It's so nice to see you, Jack," Halcie said.

Strickland put a hand on King's shoulder. "I want you to ask her when's she going to move out here; get some sun."

Halcie laughed and shook her head. "For what — twenty years now, Arthur, you've been saying the same thing. It may surprise you to hear the sun still does shine in New York."

"It's not the same thing. The sun out here" — Strickland paused, searching for words — "it gives you a *California* tan."

Halcie and King both laughed, and then Strickland, who hadn't been aware he'd made a humorous remark until their reaction, laughed, too, before he moved away toward the front door again, where more guests were arriving. He was followed close behind by a huge, muscular-looking man Halcie had noticed earlier. The man was standing behind Strickland at the door when she entered the house and behind him again later, when the producer led her over to Jack King.

She made a motion with her hand toward the man and asked King. "Who's he?"

King made a joke of his answer. "I could tell you that possibly Arthur didn't think he cast a large enough shadow so he hired one . . ."

Halcie gave King a warning arched-eyebrow look. "Jack!"

King smiled ". . . but of course I won't tell you that." He lowered his voice. "Actually, although not too many people know this, the guy's Arthur's bodyguard."

Halcie was astonished. "Bodyguard! You're serious, aren't you? Why in the world would

13

Arthur need a bodyguard?"

"It seems," King said, voice still low, "Arthur's been receiving anonymous death threats. Letters. He took them to the police. I gather they didn't take the threats too seriously. But Arthur did. So he hired a bodyguard. Paulie Bianco's his name. Arthur tells most people Paulie's his new chauffeur."

"And Arthur doesn't know who's sending the letters?" Halcie asked.

"He says not." King shook his head and added, "You could take your pick from a possible cast of thousands, I suppose."

Halcie laughed.

"So," King said, "how's New York City other than that the sun does shine there?"

"Haven't you heard? They're still building it," she answered. "Higher, longer, wider. And with it all, most people there complain they can't find a place to live. Don't be surprised if any day now they level Central Park, fill in the Hudson and the East rivers, and put up buildings where they were."

He grinned. "But still you stay there."

"It's my home," she said. She glanced around the room. "Is Joan here tonight? I always liked her."

"I haven't seen her," King said. "She and Arthur are still separated. She's living in the

14

house in Palm Springs, he's living here. I don't know whether she was invited tonight."

Halcie continued to glance around the room. "If she wasn't, it looks like everyone else in Hollywood was, and came."

"Yeah. Like the old studio slogan used to proclaim: 'There are more stars here than there are in the heavens.' Who'd pass up a party thrown by — after tomorrow night — the producer of the best picture of the year?"

"You're that certain *The Amulet*'s going to win?"

"Let me put it to you this way," King said and winked, "if coercion, bribery, flattery, and the most expensive ad campaign ever run in the trades — all of it Arthur's doing — can swing it, the picture's got a lock on the award."

The orchestra on the terrace was playing, slow tempo, "These Foolish Things."

Jim Edgell, leaning against one of the tent poles set up around the dance floor, listened to the music and thought: *A Yank in the RAF.* Tyrone Power. He'd seen the movie on TV again a few weeks earlier. The song was the theme music for the film.

Edgell had just gone out onto the terrace and lit a cigarette to get away from the crush of people in the living room, almost every one

15

of whom had approached him to congratulate him on the screenplay for *The Amulet* and his Academy Award nomination. This was his first real Hollywood party, and no doubt about it, it was a heady sensation to be congratulated by a roomful of celebrated people the rest of the world had to stand in line and pay to see.

He took a drag on his cigarette and looked in through the French doors to see if Courtney Ware had arrived yet. He couldn't spot her. He accepted a glass of champagne from a passing waiter, drank, and reflected on the curious successes and failures of his life as a writer that had brought him to this night.

Two years earlier, when he was thirty-four years old, he was living in New York City, where he was a modestly successful author of what are called, in publishing, mid-list books, meaning books that sell between twenty-five and fifty thousand copies in hard cover. In seven years he had published six novels, some of which had sold better than others, all of which had been reprinted in paperback, all of which had been *optioned* for motion pictures – some optioned over and over again, year after year.

For seven years there were meetings and drinks and lunches and, sometimes, breakfasts with lawyers and agents and producers or producers' representatives, a couple of times with directors, twice with stars themselves who were looking for properties. There were option contracts drawn and signed and option money paid, there were actual scripts written by screenwriters from his novels, but no movies made.

Edgell, who had always been interested in films almost as much as he was in books, had finally given up believing he would ever see any of his own work on the screen. And begun believing he didn't give a damn.

And then came the telephone call from Arthur Strickland in Hollywood. He knew who Strickland was; there had been articles about him in *The New York Times* and a profile in *People* magazine, "The Hottest Producer in Hollywood."

"Listen," Strickland said in the phone call, "I've got this story I want you to write a screenplay for. A love story. The kind of story you did in your novel *Choices of the Heart*. I liked that one."

Strickland wanted him to leave for the coast the next day. (Later, when Edgell and Jack King became friends and Edgell told the story of that phone call, the director said, "You see, he was conditioning you from the outset about the Hollywood way of doing things, where it's

'Hurry up – and hurry up!' ")

The next day Edgell flew to L. A.

Strickland had his own production offices in a building on the Centurion Studios lot in Culver City. Two days after the phone call, Edgell met with him there, in an office larger than the co-op apartment Edgell lived in in New York. The office had a split decor, with Strickland's desk as the dividing line. The desk itself, the producer's chair, the furnishings behind it – cabinets, lamps, bar – were all as outsized as the enormous room, while arranged in front of the desk were a dozen low chairs that would have been a tight squeeze for any person weighing twenty-five pounds more than Edgell's weight of one forty-five.

Later, when he thought back over that first meeting, Edgell was amazed at how little had been said, almost all of it by Strickland.

The producer already had had Edgell's contract drawn up: $150,000 for the script, payable by a third upon signing, a third on delivery of an approved script, a third on the first day of principal photography, plus 2 percent of the net. Strickland did not want him to sign then. He told Edgell to have his agent go over the contract and talk to Strickland's lawyers.

Edgell was equally amazed when he discovered there was no book, no story on paper, for him to turn into a script. Strickland simply talked the idea for a film to be called *The Amulet*. The story, he explained, would be set in a small town in Arizona and on an Indian reservation near the town. The time would be the present and the 1920's.

In the present the heroine, in her eighties, is an artist whose powerful, primitive paintings have made her world-famous. Although a white woman (and still quite beautiful), she lives in a small house on the reservation with the Indians, who revere her. She is teacher and doctor to them, as well as a renowned artist who has chosen for her subjects the desert, the Indians themselves, and their ceremonial objects, customs, and dress. Her masterpiece is a painting called "The Amulet." It is of a dazzling charm hung on an gold chain, set against a backdrop of two towering mountain peaks, so the effect achieved is of the amulet resting in the cleavage between two exquisitely formed breasts.

It would be established that each day, in the present, the heroine makes a ritual pilgrimage into the nearby small village, usually accompanied by one or two Indian children walking through the town square where she is acknowledged with respect, to the cemetery, where she places the fresh-cut flowers she carries at a tombstone.

The film would then flash back to the 1920's, where the heroine is seen as a beautiful young girl. She belongs to one of the leading families in town, her father a prominent judge. She is courted by all the single men in the village until she meets and falls in love with a new-comer. The two are inseparable, and on the night he proposes to her and she accepts he slips an amulet on a chain around her neck. He tells her it is the visible symbol of his love for her and that it will always protect her.

They announce plans for their wedding, and there are scenes of them at grand parties and dances, at picnics, enjoying an affluent, carefree life.

This life in the town is in dramatic contrast to the poverty of the Indians on the nearby reservation. The townspeople are indifferent to the plight of the Indians although when one or another of them gets into trouble in town and is arrested and brought before the judge, the heroine's father, he is compassionate and fair to them.

A few days before the heroine and the young man are to be married, he goes off to fish alone in a river outside town. There is a violent rainstorm. He doesn't return. A search party goes to look for him. His capsized boat and fishing gear are found, but there is no sign of him even though the searchers drag the river.

The heroine is devastated. Even though there's no body to bury, she insists upon a funeral service and picks the tombstone to mark his grave. Every day thereafter she visits the grave, wearing the amulet and bringing fresh-cut flowers.

Meanwhile there has occurred an outbreak of deadly smallpox on the reservation, which is quarantined from the townspeople. There are deaths and burials daily.

In the town all the single young men again try to court the heroine, but she rejects them. Then, one late afternoon, the young man thought to be dead appears at the heroine's house. He tries to explain to her that on the day of the storm, when his boat capsized in the river, he simply disappeared because he was afraid of getting married. Now he has returned, having decided he can't live without her.

She is shocked, humiliated, furious with him. She gets her father's shotgun, fires and kills him, then collapses.

Her mother calls the judge, who comes home, hears the whole story, then calls in the chief of police, the coroner and the town's prosecutor. Much as the judge loves his daughter, he says she must stand trial. The chief of police, the coroner, and the prosecutor all try to convince him that she should be spared the disgrace of a public trial. Together they will secretly bury the young man's body in the cemetery where his tombstone already stands. No one else in town need know what has happened.

Reluctantly the judge agrees, but insists that there must be a secret trial held in his courtroom in the dead of night. The others can argue his daughter's defense, but he will pass final judgment.

At night they bury the body. The heroine takes off the amulet and buries it at the foot of the tombstone. Later a trial is held in the deserted courthouse, and the judge pronounces sentence: His daughter must go to live on the quarantined Indian reservation and help tend to the victims suffering from smallpox. If she herself survives, she must stay until the deadly epidemic ends.

She goes to the reservation, nurses the victims, teaches the children, helps bury the dead — and begins to paint. She survives, the epidemic ends, but she stays on, even after the death of her parents.

In the final scene the heroine carries flowers to the cemetery again, and this time digs up the amulet and brushes the dirt away. As she places the amulet around her neck, the scene dissolves to the scene in the painting, the dazzling charm on a gold chain set against the backdrop of two towering mountain peaks.

Strickland wanted the script written quickly. He could get the legendary Halcyon Harper to play the heroine when she is older. In addition, he had Kathleen Havens, one of the big names at the moment, under contract to star in a film for him. He wanted the film to be *The Amulet*. It was important, he said, that production begin within a few months.

Edgell knew, from experience with plot ideas he'd turned into novels, that he could do the script. It didn't matter that the idea hadn't originated with him; in the writing he would make the work his own.

Strickland offered him an office at the studio, but Edgell wanted someplace where he would be completely alone. He went down to Laguna Beach, an area he liked when he'd visited California before, and which was not that far from Hollywood. He found a small house to rent there, one room, kitchen, and bath, on a cliff overlooking the ocean.

There was nothing to distract him, and framed by the picture window was the natural seascape outside to soothe him. He finished the script in six weeks. Strickland approved the first draft and hired Jack King to direct.

Soon afterward, preproduction was started on the film: casting, building sets, and selecting locations. Edgell's presence was not required until the actual shooting was under way.

Finally, then, filming began — and, three weeks into it, shut down; there were some problems with Kathleen Havens, and a week passed before shooting resumed after Strickland brought in a newcomer, Courtney Ware, to star.

All through the writing of the script Edgell had an image in his mind of how each character looked, as he did of all the characters he created in his works. He tried not to have his characters resemble people he knew or knew about; it was his theory that then the characters would have no freedom to become themselves, even if on paper. Because of this, while he was writing *The Amulet,* he blocked out any image of Kathleen Havens as the heroine, even though he knew she had been cast to play the role.

The image he did have, had had through the weeks he had spent writing the script, was — shocking to him when he was finally introduced to her — Courtney Ware. Later he would think that for him it was a case of love *before* first sight. A doomed love, he would subsequently discover; she was married and, so it seemed, very much in love with her husband.

What was even more unbearable to Edgell

was that the man she had married was perceived as a cretinous bore by all who met him. Richard Dald had the boyish-beyond-his-years look of an aging juvenile actor, with a full head of blond hair and the fair, smooth skin of his face to his advantage but with, to his disadvantage, what had once been baby fat now indulgent, thirtyish plumpness. He was a self-important would-be playwright with no talent. He never stopped talking about himself and the play he was writing, and on the days he would bring Courtney to the set or pick her up he drove everyone crazy.

(Jack King's observation of the marriage was: "There's no way of explaining it, unless she's like some women in this world who blindly marry the first man who makes love to them. You could say, in a poke she bought a pig.")

The orchestra on the terrace segued from "These Foolish Things" into "Mood Indigo."

Edgell heard the sound of scattered applause from the living room, and he walked across the terrace to the French doors. He could see that at the opposite end of the room, Courtney had just arrived. She made her entrance on the arm of Eddie McCoy, the press agent for Arthur G. Strickland Productions.

The simple, sleek black evening gown she wore was artfully designed to show off the amulet on the gold chain around her neck, a present from Strickland and something of a trademark of hers since the release of the film. Edgell was pleased to see that on the third finger of her left hand was the matching ring he had given her.

Strickland followed her from the door as she made her way into the room, pausing to hug Halcie Harper and to kiss Jack King on the cheek. Eddie McCoy and Strickland then led her through the crowd to a corner of the room where Trish Sutherland, Hollywood correspondent for *The New York Times,* was waiting to interview her.

Edgell, watching from the terrace, enjoyed the simple sight of Courtney: the prettiness of her, yes, but something more — the image of graceful motion and shape her body projected, a certain balance of head and shoulders, hips and legs when she walked, a certain beauty of form, head and shoulders, hips and legs when she was still.

He turned away and went in search of another glass of champagne.

2

Trish Sutherland held up the microphone to the small tape recorder.

"Tell me, Miss Ware, is it true, as you were once quoted as saying, that you were unhappy with your role in *The Amulet*?"

"That is not quite an accurate quote. The next part of what I said was left out. What I said next was that I was afraid I wasn't experienced enough to do the role as well as it should be done. I had just started work on the movie at the time."

"But there were problems with the making of the picture?"

"I'm told there are almost always problems with the making of pictures: that it's the end result that counts."

"And how do you feel about it now?"

"If the Motion Picture Academy has decided I did well enough to honor me with an Oscar nomination, well, obviously, I'm pleased."

Strickland had walked away after delivering Courtney to the interviewer, while McCoy remained to listen in until he could see how the exchange was going. Now he tuned out and relaxed. He was pleased that Courtney had learned from his coaching how to field questions from the media, a problem she'd had in her early days in Hollywood.

Eddie McCoy, short, rotund, in his sixties, and always impeccably tailored, had been the press agent for Arthur G. Strickland Productions since the company's inception. Before that, he was a Broadway press agent and later a press agent with MGM, Paramount, and a couple of other independent producers.

Some months earlier, when principal photography had started on *The Amulet*, there were problems with Kathleen Havens, who had the lead role. The way Eddie heard the story was that she wanted more money and wanted her part expanded. To force her demands, during the first three weeks of shooting, she was uncooperative with the director and twice walked off the set.

At the time, Eddie was in New York on vacation. Strickland phoned him there and instructed him to find an actress named Courtney Ware, who lived in the Soho section of Manhattan; he had come across a photograph of her in the Centurion Studio's casting files.

Strickland wanted Eddie to offer her a screen test and bring her to Hollywood right away. He told Eddie he'd decided to play hardball with Kathleen Havens. His plan was to start filming with this Courtney Ware, who somewhat resembled Kathleen Havens, in the starring role. He said he figured that once Kathleen thought she was being replaced – and that later he would sue her – she'd come to her senses and return to the film on their original terms.

None of this, of course, was to be told to the unknown Courtney Ware. Strickland assured Eddie she would get a screen test, and if everything worked out, they'd try to find a spot for her in a minor role.

Courtney Ware's address turned out to be what looked like it had once been a small parking garage. There was a cloth banner hanging over the entrance on which the hand-painted words read PRO BONO THEATER. Eddie recalled vaguely, from his high school Latin lessons, that that translated into something like "for the good" or "for the public good."

The young man who let Eddie into the building introduced himself as Richard Dald, Courtney's husband. He was clearly excited at the prospect Eddie was offering and went off to get his wife.

The interior of the building was filled with folding chairs set up in rows in front of a raised platform. A dank odor of mildew seeped up from under the floorboards. A not untypical Off-Off Broadway theater, Eddie decided. Dald disappeared behind the stage area, where apparently there were other rooms.

Eddie had a long wait before he reappeared with Courtney. Dald, who had been dressed in dirty jeans and a grimy T-shirt, had changed into a sport coat and slacks and was puffing on a pipe.

Eddie saw that he'd been kept waiting because Courtney had been making up and dressing for him. Eddie lived and worked in a town — a world — of pretty females, and he thought her good-looking enough, if not quite beautiful: slim, nicely proportioned, ash blond, the features of her face delicately shaped, her skin flawless. Her makeup and dress were all wrong to show off her looks — too much eye shadow and lipstick, the skirt and blouse too loose to do justice to her figure. But the basics were there.

She was truly astonished that anyone from Hollywood would come seeking her for a screen test. She hadn't even known that a copy of her photograph and résumé had been sent out to the studios. She guessed they had been mailed off by an agent she'd employed briefly a few months before who had since gone bankrupt.

Eddie learned that she and her husband had been in New York for a year. They'd come from Baltimore, where they'd met and married while they were both working with a little theater group. They hoped to break into show business, she as an actress and he as a playwright. In New York they'd formed the Pro Bono Playhouse with some other young people. The two of them lived in a room there, and both worked part-time at a videocassette rental shop in Greenwich Village. Such shops around the city were rapidly replacing waitressing and department-store clerking in providing jobs for aspiring actors, actresses, and playwrights in Manhattan.

She was sweetly shy and hesitant at the prospect of going to Hollywood, but her husband was enthusiastic, with the understanding that he accompany her. Eddie, knowing he had no choice, agreed. Two days later the three of them left for California.

There, Eddie turned the two over to Maggie Geneen, who was Arthur Strickland's assistant. She found the couple a small apartment on

Franklin Avenue in Hollywood, and for a while after that Eddie was busy with other matters.

He did hear, however, that Jack King had made a test of Courtney and, still later, that the director was going through the motions of shooting *The Amulet* with Courtney as the heroine, the charade Strickland had planned to scare Kathleen Havens into returning to the movie. Only a couple of people in the company – none of the actors – knew what was going on.

A week or so after that, Eddie heard that Strickland's ploy seemed to have worked: Kathleen's agent had made overtures to Strickland indicating the actress would like to settle their differences and resume her role in *The Amulet*.

When Eddie received a phone call from Strickland's secretary late one afternoon telling him he was expected at a meeting in the screening room, he supposed it meant the announcement would be made that Kathleen had returned to work in the film.

Assembled in the small studio screening room when Eddie arrived were Jack King, Jim Edgell, Ben Cullin, Arthur G. Strickland vice president of production, and Herman Wolfe, AGS chief counsel. Strickland appeared, followed by Maggie Geneen, as Eddie slid into a seat.

King, it turned out, had called the meeting, which surprised Eddie. He made a brief statement, saying he wanted all of them to see something.

The lights went down, and onto the screen came a close-up of Courtney Ware's face. More footage of her followed: a two-shot of her with Robert Jason, who had been cast as the boyfriend in *The Amulet*; a medium-long shot of her surrounded by a group of young Indian children in a schoolroom; a montage of close-ups of her face as she laughed, wept, reflected sadness, then bewilderment.

The reel ended, the lights came on, and even before the first word was spoken in the screening room, there was not a single person present who didn't recognize that they had just witnessed the discovery of an extraordinary screen presence in the person of Courtney Ware.

King said simply that she was perfect for the role.

Strickland, uncharacteristically, agreed.

There was a brief discussion of how to dispose of Kathleen Havens and of drawing up a new contract for Courtney, both matters referred by Strickland to Herman Wolfe. The meeting ended with King's pronouncement that "The camera never lies; a star is born."

McCoy would always remember thinking at

that moment that it was all still true about the magic of Hollywood: A future Lana Turner could still be found at a drugstore soda fountain or a future Ava Gardner discovered through a photograph displayed in a New York shop window. It was still a town and a business where stardust could shower upon an unknown whose picture had been stuck away in a studio casting file.

"Listen to this. When I finally got in to see him, after weeks of trying to arrange a meeting, I couldn't understand what the hell he was talking about. 'Look-a,' he says, 'you want-a me to put-a money in your movie, I got-a know. Can-na it be a Roman-a numerals?' He saw I didn't follow him, so he adds, 'Roman-a numerals, like-a *Rocky the Three*, a *Godfather the Two*, like-a that.' I knew then that what I was going to answer was a mistake, but I couldn't resist it. 'Like-a *Henry the Eighth*?' I say straight-faced. 'Yeah, you-a got it!' he says. Later, somebody must have wised him up to my put-on answer. I couldn't reach him on the phone and he never returned my calls."

Maggie Geneen had gone to the powder room on the second floor of Strickland's house, and on her return paused at the top of the curving staircase overlooking the living room. From there she had what she thought of as a camera-boom view of the guests below.

Kathleen Havens had arrived downstairs while Maggie was in the powder room, and Maggie could see that most of the other guests were whispering among themselves that the actress was there. Everybody in town knew that she and Strickland were engaged in a bitter court battle over the loss of the leading role in *The Amulet*. She had not been invited to this party, but had been brought by Milton Golub, called by many one of the most powerful agents in the industry, who *was* invited. Strickland played the gracious host.

It was just such an incident, and the gossip about it, Maggie thought, that would help make the party a success.

Maggie herself liked to remain anonymous at such affairs, the observer from the sidelines of Hollywood's main action, reporting back to Strickland what she had seen and heard that he might have missed.

That she succeeded in her desire to go unnoticed most of the time was due in large part to the appearance she deliberately affected. Dressing as she did, in businesslike tailored skirts and jackets and high-necked blouses, detracted from what was, at age thirty, a knockout figure underneath. Her face, which was too plain of itself, would have been attractive enough with a little help from cosmetics and without the horn-rimmed glasses she didn't need but wore.

Another reason for this calculated camouflage was to discourage any man not discerning enough and determined enough to discover the truth of her passionate sexuality for himself. And only one man had ever succeeded.

Right after graduation from UCLA, she had gone to work for Arthur Strickland, as a secretary when he was still an agent, a reader when he became a talent packager, and finally, as his assistant when he set up as an independent producer. They became lovers during the second of her jobs.

She rather liked the arrangement, both the work and after hours. Vaguely, she imagined the day would come when Arthur would divorce his wife and marry her. She figured the odds were in her favor; Arthur had been married only once. She was patient, she could wait.

What she hadn't anticipated was the jinx that seemed to surround the making of *The Amulet*, a jinx that she felt at one point might destroy everyone connected with the production.

Replacing Kathleen Havens as the star was only the beginning of the troubles.

Casting Courtney Ware in the part was the

next problem. Perfect as she was for the picture — and no one doubted that she was destined to be a big star — she brought an excess of emotional and physical baggage to the film.

Almost immediately after she signed a new contract, and Maggie had found an oceanfront house in Malibu for her and her husband and moved them in, there was the difficulty Courtney had in accepting her new status as an overnight success. Instead of gaining confidence and enjoying her big break, the young actress became insecure and withdrawn.

Strickland and Jack King and just about everyone else on the set tried to help her, while shooting slowed down, but it was Halcie Harper who wisely found the right words. Maggie heard the story from Jack King.

One afternoon Halcie took Courtney to the Getty Museum in Malibu, and while they walked and viewed the art, Halcie talked. She said she knew how Courtney felt, suddenly finding herself a star. She wanted to tell a story, she said, a story about herself, a long time ago. She was twenty years old and had been cast in a Broadway play called *Tippy*, which had been adapted from a novel.

Just before the play was to open, when the producers were preparing to put the name up on the marquee in lights, they realized the name of the author of the novel, Agnes Morse Keller, was three words. And the name of the playwright who had adapted it, Allan Stephen Ruston, was also three words. That was too much for the marquee to accommodate.

All the producers had that would fit was the title of the play, *Tippy*, and another short name. So they decided that what would go on the marquee was "Halcyon Harper in *Tippy*."

That was how she became a star overnight, Halcie told Courtney. A true story. She added that of course what had happened was simply luck, just as what had happened to Courtney was simply luck. Some people scoff at the idea that luck can play a role in life, Halcie said. But then, she was an actress before she became a star. Courtney was an actress before she was chosen for *The Amulet*. Halcie said luck is when the pieces one has already created come together to form a design and that Courtney should accept that and go forward with her life, just as she had done.

There was no more slowdowns on the filming because of Courtney's insecurity, but then there was the problem of her husband.

Taking advantage of his wife's privileged position, Dald began spending all his time on the set when they were shooting, always talking about himself and the play he was writing, or suggesting ideas for movies he would write. He would go on endlessly to King, Strickland, Edgell, Maggie, the assistant director, Mark Whelan, whenever he could corner them.

Courtney was embarrassed by her husband's boorishness, although she tried not to show it in front of him. The others were annoyed while attempting to put up with him. When, as was inevitable, his presence on the set began to adversely affect shooting, Strickland had to tell him that he was no longer welcome.

The producer took Dald aside and tried to tell him quietly. Dald exploded in anger, screaming at Strickland, threatening that he would take Courtney back to New York and the film would be ruined. The confrontation between the two men was loud and bitter, and everyone working on the set heard it.

Strickland lost his temper and shouted back that Dald would ruin his wife's career, that he had no talent, and that he was to be barred from the studio in the future. Dald stormed away. Courtney, who was in the middle of filming a scene, burst into tears. Shooting was suspended, and Strickland arranged to have his chauffeur drive her home to Malibu.

The following day Courtney was late arriving on the set, and her face was swollen and puffy from weeping. The company managed to complete a couple of scenes, and Strickland sent Courtney home early again.

Most of the crew was still on the set an hour or so later when Strickland received a frantic phone call from Courtney, saying that her husband had committed suicide. He had left a note telling her he was going to swim out into the ocean and drown. She had found his robe at the edge of the beach.

Strickland, Maggie, King, and Edgell rushed out to the house in Malibu. The police had to be called, and divers were sent out to search for the body, but it was never recovered.

"The son of a bitch couldn't even think of an original way to commit suicide!" Strickland raged to Maggie later. "He had to do an imitation of Norman Maine in *A Star Is Born*."

After a memorial service for Dald, Courtney had a nervous breakdown. Strickland had her spirited away to a hospital he knew out in the desert. For a couple of weeks the doctor there kept her on uppers and downers so she couldn't think of anything, much less her grief. Then she was checked out and returned to work on *The Amulet*.

Edgell, who — as everyone in the company knew — was in love with Courtney, was with her constantly for a time thereafter.

During all this turmoil, there was another

problem on the picture: Robert Jason, playing the role of the boyfriend, began to complain that he was being neglected and his lines were being cut while more lines in the script were being added for Courtney. He said he felt like an extra.

Jason had been an actor almost all his life, as a child, as a juvenile and, in recent years, as a young leading man. But he hadn't done a movie for a long time before he was cast in *The Amulet*, and he had taken the job knowing it was not a starring role. Still, when so much attention was being paid to Courtney, he began to protest.

Jason had other difficulties as well, in his personal life. He was drinking heavily, and he and his wife had separated. Ten days before the picture was completed, he failed to turn up on the set. King had finished filming Jason but he needed him to dub some lines on the sound track.

Strickland dispatched Maggie and a driver to Jason's house in Benedict Canyon. He figured the actor had a hangover.

Maggie and the driver found that Jason had been drinking all right, apparently the night before. The front door to the house was unlocked, and inside Jason lay sprawled at the foot of the stairs, dead, his neck broken, an empty quart bottle of vodka near where the body rested.

Again, the police had to be called, and Strickland and Herman Wolfe went to the house and called Jason's estranged wife in Santa Barbara, where she was living.

Later Strickland would say, "Another one, this time doing a takeoff of Don Birnam in *The Lost Weekend*. What the hell is going on?"

Jason's widow, Vicky, was full of grief and anger, and accused Strickland of causing her husband's death by demeaning him during the filming of *The Amulet*, and even of being responsible for Jason's drinking and their separation.

"Can you believe it!" Strickland complained to Maggie later. "Why, hell, everybody knows Jason's been a souse ever since he was old enough to buy a drink. And she — everybody knows she's slept around everywhere . . . from Burbank to Santa Barbara."

Strickland's real worry was that Jason's death would cast a pall over the picture and the public would stay away from it in the proverbial droves.

His other problem was that, with all the delays in filming, the production of the film was over budget, with the final cut still to be made, and he was strapped for cash.

He and his wife, Joan, were separated by then and planning a divorce. She had plenty of money of her own, and they had worked out a divorce settlement that included a percentage of the gross of *The Amulet* to go to her.

In a bind for financing, Strickland had gone to Joan for funds. He told her that if he couldn't raise the money he needed, the film would never be released and she would lose any chance she might have to cash in on her percentage. He offered her additional points of the gross in exchange for more capital. Her lawyer and Strickland's personal lawyer, Henry Bickle, put together a deal in which Strickland gave up a large share of his percentage and she advanced him the money he required to complete the picture and release it.

Maggie had had to play nursemaid to Courtney, to Jason, and to Strickland during the production, and at the end had to accept the fact that Strickland's divorce would be delayed until the film went into release.

At the wrap party for *The Amulet* practically everybody believed the picture was going to be a bomb.

Now, standing at the top of the stairs in Strickland's house, Maggie thought she had never dreamed there would be a night and a party like this one, celebrating the commercial and critical success of the film, and the possibility that the next night it might win several Academy Awards. The thought occurred to her that the story of the production of the film might have made a better movie than the one they'd shot. She was reminded of Jack King's remark when, after all the headaches they'd had, the nominations were announced: "It just goes to prove there's no show like show business."

"You know that new hot shot agent in town, Buddy Everts? He was handling this actor Jack King had turned down for his next picture. Buddy, arguing the actor had dramatic talent, says to Jack, 'Even granting that he's no Larry Oliver.' And Jack says, 'You remember the names of The Three Stooges?' Buddy thinks and says, 'Yeah, Larry, Moe, and Curly.' 'Well,' Jack says, 'a better way to put it about your guy's dramatic talent is, even granting he's no Larry Three Stooges.' "

Edgell came back into the living room carrying two glasses of champagne as Courtney finished her interview with Trish Sutherland.

When Courtney started to move away, he hurried over, offering her one of the glasses of champagne. She hesitated for a moment, then accepted, looking at him, not smiling, as she nodded. "Thank you, Jim."

She turned to walk away and he put out a hand, touching her wrist. "I have to talk to you. Please," he said, his voice a hoarse whisper.

She looked at him for a moment before she nodded. "I'm going up to the powder room to freshen my makeup. Wait a few minutes and come up."

He watched her walk away and up the stairs.

"Jim, lad, how's the scribbling going?" Eddie McCoy asked, suddenly standing beside him.

"Eddie, hi!" Edgell said. "The script's coming along okay."

"Arthur's anxious to move fast now," McCoy said, "Cash in on *The Amulet*."

"It'll be ready in time." Edgell took a step to leave.

"Arthur's predicting you're writing another hit."

Edgell liked McCoy, but he wanted to get away now and up to Courtney. "I hope I don't disappoint him," he said and then, "Excuse me, Eddie. We'll have a long talk soon."

Edgell left quickly and went up the stairs. He passed Maggie on the way up as she was coming down, and they exchanged friendly hellos, she smiling quizzically but saying nothing, although he knew she must have seen

Courtney go upstairs and must know he was going to her.

The door to the powder room was closed and he tapped on it softly. Courtney opened it and, after he went in, closed the door again.

"Well, Jim," she said and motioned to a small cushioned seat near the washbasin. He sat down.

She had filled the basin with water and scrubbed all the makeup from her face, a ritual he had watched her perform at other times, when she put on fresh makeup. She looked very young and vulnerable, her face, when she turned back to the mirror, like a photograph that might have been taken of her long before that face became the face of the star of *The Amulet*.

He had had this disquieting experience with her before; an altering of appearance or, more often, of mood, when she seemed to slip elusively just out of focus in front of his eyes. He lit a cigarette.

After Dald's suicide and her breakdown, Edgell had been there to comfort her. She had accepted him gratefully, needed and wanted him there. He was already in love with her and, he began to believe, she was in love with him. She moved into the small house in Laguna with him.

Edgell was happy all the time. They saw no one else. They swam in the ocean, took long walks, she read his novels, he started writing a new movie script, they watched rented movies on the VCR most nights, and later most nights made love.

She waited a long time before, one day, she gave him a large cardboard box she'd brought with her. She told him it contained the play Dald had been writing. She hadn't been able to bring herself to look at it. She wanted him to read it and tell her what he thought.

She left him alone in the house and went out to do some grocery shopping.

Edgell didn't really want to read the play. He didn't know what his feelings would be if it turned out to be a brilliant work of art, and he didn't know how she would feel, or feel about him, if he had to tell her it was no good.

There were over a thousand typed pages in the box — she had told him Dald kept all the pages he'd revised — and as he started reading through them he was at first baffled, then astonished. There was no play, only a single page that Dald had rewritten over a thousand times, changing dialogue, the names of the characters, the directions but always Page 1, Act I, Scene 1.

Edgell didn't know how Courtney would

react when he had to tell her. He was relieved when she simply shook her head sadly and, telling him she wanted to be alone for a while, went out and down to the beach. He watched her from the window.

She walked out to the edge of the sand, carrying the pages from the box, and threw them, a few pages at a time, into the ocean until they all disappeared.

Afterward, when she returned, she was very loving to him, and neither of them ever discussed the incident again.

During the days they were together in Laguna, *The Amulet* was going through the final cut, and no one from the production company bothered them.

In December the film opened and was an immediate critical and box office success. Both of them were in constant demand — she more than he of course — to do interviews, and she to make public appearances. They also began receiving offers to do other films. Strickland had an option on both of them for another film, and once *The Amulet* was a hit, he exercised his option. Edgell continued to work on his original screenplay, which Courtney would star in.

She was away much of the time and soon was staying in her house in Malibu when she was in town. Edgell had spent the greater portion of his life alone, as most writers do, are forced to do in order to work, and had never been bothered by being alone. But the emptiness she left gave him a new sense of loneliness: the particular absence of a particular person. He was distracted, restlessly unhappy, his mind obsessed with missing her.

Now, in the powder room at Strickland's house, she had laid out all her makeup articles, and as she began to touch up her face, closely examining her reflection in the mirror, she asked, "How have you been?"

He tried to keep his tone bantering. " 'There's just me and my shadow.' Or, if I'm out, 'I walk alone.' 'I think of you night and day.' You know, all those sad lyrics they sing is how I've been. I miss you."

"I'm sorry, Jim. Truly." She was looking at him in the mirror, and the real concern in her voice made him momentarily happy. "It's just been a terribly busy time. Promoting the movie, the interviews, the traveling. I thought you'd understand."

He nodded. "That I understand. What I can't is not being able to reach you on the phone, with either Maggie screening your calls or that damn answering machine. Or why you haven't returned my calls or answered my letters. Or when I go to your house and you're not home."

"Most of the time I'm not." She was putting on eye shadow and was silent, concentrating. Then she said, "And I was going to answer your letters, call you — in time."

She was silent again, carefully smoothing on lip gloss, brushing her eyebrows with a fingertip, dusting her cheeks with light blush powder.

He was silent, too, engrossed in observing how each brush tip applied to the reflection in the mirror brought the face he knew into ever clearer view.

"There!" she said finally, turning toward him.

He stubbed out his cigarette in an ashtray next to the cushioned seat, reached and pulled her to him, his arms around her hips. He rested his head against her. She stood still, not yielding, not resisting.

"That's not it at all — what you said, is it?" he asked miserably. "It's Arthur's doing, isn't it? He thinks we're not good for one another. That's what he told me. I'm sure he told you, too."

"He told me that, yes," she said. "Not that we weren't good for one another, exactly. But for now that neither of us should be distracted by personal involvements."

"Then it is Arthur!" Edgell said.

Courtney touched the top of his head tenderly. "It's not just Arthur. I need some time. You were so patient, so loving, so understanding before. Give me some time."

When he didn't answer, she pulled away from his embrace gently.

"I have to go," she said. "Please don't be too unhappy."

And she was gone.

A few minutes before midnight, when the faint notes of the tune the orchestra on the terrace was playing, "Someone to Watch Over Me," could be heard in the living room, Joan Strickland came in the door, her choice of escort creating the second scene that would be a subject of gossip for some days around town.

Marty Cowell and Arthur Strickland once were partners in a production company the two of them had formed. They had a falling out after each had accused the other of cheating on a split of profits from their only film, and had not spoken to one another in some years.

When Strickland reached the door, no one else at the party was close enough to overhear the conversation among the three of them, but practically everyone in the room witnessed the scene as it was played out in pantomime.

There was much animated arguing, and some

gesturing and shoving, Strickland red-faced with anger, Joan all pretended wide-eyed innocence, Cowell grinning in amusement, until finally Paulie Bianco was there, gently propelling Joan and Cowell out the door.

No one present relished the scene as much as nationally syndicated columnist Didi Jones, who stood back out of the way and quickly wrote the words that would lead off her column the next day in newspapers from coast to coast:

FIREWORKS GALORE at the California-chic party thrown last night in Hollywood by film producer Arthur Strickland to celebrate the Academy Awards nominations for his film "The Amulet." Arthur's estranged wife, Joan, showed up with Arthur's ex-partner, Marty Cowell (the two men have been at odds for years), setting off an explosion of gesturing and shoving before the two guests were forcibly ejected. Although what the three said couldn't be heard, if body language could kill there would have been three bodies on the floor of Arthur's Bel Air mansion.

3

The next morning, the day of the annual Academy Awards, the sky above Los Angeles was overcast with a fine, gray mist drifting in off the Pacific to the southwest.

Laura Harrow's estate on seven acres in Beverly Hills had been a Hollywood showcase ever since the days of the first talking pictures, when Laura was one of the biggest stars of the screen and had first lived there. In addition to the mansion itself, there were two guest houses surrounding the swimming pool, tennis courts, a separate building containing a screening room, and a garden. A high stone wall circled the grounds, and in recent years the wrought-iron gates at the front of the stone wall was manned by security guards around the clock.

Halcie Harper and Laura Harrow had been close friends from the time they both starred in early sound movies at the old New Arts Studio, run by Nat Holman.

Halcie, who was already an established star on Broadway at the time, came to Hollywood with her husband, David Martin, a best-selling novelist and for a while a screenwriter at New Arts. Halcie was then offered her first starring role in a film by Holman. Laura's husband, Fred Turman, was a top producer at New Arts, and Halcie, David, Laura, and Fred went almost everywhere together, including their vacations.

In recent years, whenever Halcie returned from New York on brief trips, such as for the night's Awards, she stayed at Laura's estate.

On this morning Halcie was awakened when the maid brought her breakfast tray. On the tray was a note from Laura:

Good morning, Dear Halcie!
I hope you slept well and enjoyed the party last night. I want a full account of everything that happened! I know you have a brunch to attend and a busy day and night. I shall be watching you on television tonight when you accept your award.
Love, L.H.

Halcie finished reading the note, shook her head, and laughed. Dear, dear Laura.
How she wished the two of them could sit

down with tea, or a bottle of bourbon, and gossip as they used to do in the old days, and laugh at the absurdity of the experiences they had had in the business.

In fact, it was just an absurd experience that had brought them together in the beginning.

Halcie had just made her first picture, a New Arts production, and had won an Academy Award for Best Actress.

The next day Nat Holman called her into his office at the studio. At that time he was the most successful, and most autocratic, studio head in Hollywood, as famous as most of the stars he had under contract.

Laura was in the office, made up for a film that was shooting that day. It was the first time the two actresses met, Halcie the biggest star on Broadway, Laura the biggest star in Hollywood, a real beauty who was, that day, dressed in a very seductive gown she was to wear in her film.

After Holman introduced the two, he explained to Halcie that he wanted to make a screen test of her wearing a version of the gown Laura had on. A sexy dress, he explained.

Halcie agreed that the gown was sexy, but she added, "Mr. Holman, you can put me in that dress and you can make all the screen tests you want of me, but you're not going to see anything different from what you see right now looking at me."

Holman had nodded his head sadly, leaned back in his chair, and said very seriously, "Then, Halcie, I guess you're just going to have to *act*."

At that point Halcie and Laura both had what sounded like a coughing fit, which continued until they left Holman's office, then outside, beyond his hearing, turned into gales of laughter, each hanging onto the other. From that moment on they were close friends.

Now Halcie went to the window of her room overlooking the estate's garden. Sometimes when she was visiting she was able to spot Laura in the garden. And though Laura always had a veil covering her face, Halcie took pleasure in seeing her, even from a distance.

Laura hadn't allowed anyone to see her in person since she'd made her last film and retired almost thirty years before, soon after her husband died. She wanted people to remember her the way she looked when she was a star, and she made no exception to the rule, not even Halcie. The two talked on the phone several times a week when Halcie was in New York and sometimes exchanged letters, and when Halcie visited could only communicate the same way.

This day Laura was nowhere to be seen in the garden. Halcie moved away from the window. She had to leave soon for a late-morning brunch with Arthur Strickland, Jack King, and some of the others, to discuss Strickland's next film. Strickland was sending a limousine to pick her up. After brunch she had an appointment with the hairdresser, and then she had to dress for the evening's ceremonies.

Before she left, Halcie wanted to write a long note to Laura about the party the night before. Laura would thoroughly enjoy all the juicy gossip about Joan Strickland showing up with Marty Cowell, and about the appearance of Kathleen Havens. Even though Laura never went out in public and didn't know any of the people personally, she still kept up with what went on in the business. Halcie liked to amuse her old friend with any piece of gossip she picked up. It was harmless enough. As Jack King had observed years ago: "In this climate of work where you're hot one minute and cold the next, we're all susceptible; gossip is a communicable disease."

Maggie Geneen had had only four hours' sleep. When the party ended at 2 A.M., she stayed on at Strickland's house for another hour, making sure the help cleaned up all the mess. Arthur disappeared upstairs after the last guest left. She saw no more of him. At three she left his house and drove to her apartment on Wilshire Boulevard, slept for four hours, and was up again waiting in the lobby of her building when Strickland came to pick her up for the group brunch at the Polo Lounge of the Beverly Hills Hotel. Paulie Bianco was driving the black stretch Cadillac. The glass partition between front and back seats was closed.

As she settled into the backseat next to Strickland, the car phone was buzzing and Strickland was rummaging through the papers in the attaché case on his lap. The phone kept buzzing.

"You want me to answer that, Arthur?" she finally asked.

He glanced up. "What? Oh, the phone? No. It's probably Joan. She's been leaving messages on my answering machine all morning, says she wants to explain about last night. To hell with her."

Strickland went back to flipping through the papers, then said, "Where the hell's that contract? Halcie's? It's not in here."

Maggie held out a hand. "Let me look."

"It's not in there!" he said but passed the attaché case to Maggie.

She leafed through the folders, extracted a

sheaf of papers, and held them up. "There's the contract, Arthur. It was in between the pages in the status report folder."

"Well, put the contract on top," he said impatiently. He lit a cigar while Maggie closed the attaché case and placed it on the seat. The phone stopped buzzing.

Maggie glanced at him. "You could say 'Good morning,' you know."

Strickland took her hand and kissed it. "So," he said, "We didn't get to talk last night; give me a report on Courtney. You did check on her yesterday, right?"

Maggie nodded. "Just as we planned. I went to her house unannounced. About two-thirty yesterday afternoon."

"And — ?"

"Her car was in the driveway so I knew she was there. I went to the front door and rang the bell and knocked. I had to wait for a long time before she appeared."

"Did she seem surprised? Upset at seeing you?"

"Well," Maggie said, "when she opened the door, she had her pocketbook and car keys in her hand. She said she was just on her way out."

Strickland nodded. "In other words, she didn't want you to come into the house."

"Exactly," Maggie said. "But I told her I had just been to see my mother, and since I was in the neighborhood, I just stopped by to say hello. Then I told her I was sorry to detain her but that I simply *had* to use her facilities, that I was in *agony*."

Strickland patted her hand. "Smart girl." He took a puff on his cigar.

Maggie smiled. "There wasn't much she could do except let me in. But, as good an actress as she is, she couldn't conceal that she wasn't happy at my being there. She hurried me in and out."

"So you didn't really find out anything?" Strickland asked.

Maggie smiled again. "Actually, I did. There were two glasses on the coffee table in the living room. Both glasses had ice and parts of a drink in them. And someone who had just been in the room had been smoking; I could smell the odor. And she doesn't smoke. That's all I discovered. But whoever had been there — was there — was nowhere in sight."

Strickland sighed. "So she *is* seeing someone, as you suspected."

"I'd hate to think so, yes. Every time I've walked in on her unexpectedly there's been — something to suggest someone has just been there. And the feeling I get is it's been a man."

"And you don't think it's Jim Edgell?" Strickland asked.

Maggie shook her head. "I'm almost positive she's cut him off. He's too unhappy these days. I think *he'd* like to find out what's going on, what she's up to and with whom."

Strickland took another puff on his cigar and said, "But why would she be sneaking around, hiding it from everybody?"

"Maybe she's afraid that you'll disapprove. After all, you did speak to her about Jim, and to him about her, to break them up."

"That was different." Strickland let the car window down and flipped his cigar out. "I didn't want their relationship to affect the new picture. Hell, Maggie, you've been around this business long enough to know that if two people on a movie get involved, either too hot and heavy or it cools off, what they feel can make a difference in how the film turns out. That's what concerned me."

"I know you think that, Arthur. And probably you're right." Maggie shrugged.

"Damn!" Strickland said. "I have too much invested in her now to let her get all messed up emotionally this soon again. If she's seeing somebody, I have to know who it is! That means hiring somebody to watch her until I find out."

"You know your trouble, Arthur? You look upon your actors as if they were children, when what you really want is for them to behave as adults."

Strickland looked at Maggie. "My dear," he said dryly, "you have it exactly backward. They *are* children; it's when they start acting like adults that they get into trouble."

Jim Edgell hadn't wanted to drive back to Laguna after the party at Arthur Strickland's the previous night. He had rented a room at the Beverly Hills Hotel, where they were all to have brunch, and so he was the first one at the table in the Polo Lounge.

Since it was still only late morning, the booths were not yet filled by the mobs of movie people that would soon come swarming in until every seat was taken. Edgell didn't recognize any of the people who sat in two of the booths in the restaurant nor at a couple of the tables on the patio outside.

The waiter had just brought him a Bloody Mary and a pot of coffee when Halcie Harper appeared, followed soon after by Jack King, and then Herman Wolfe. They talked of matters of no consequence, awaiting Strickland's arrival. Halcie told them of her morning at Laura Harrow's house, all of them fascinated by any news of the reclusive actress. King talked of some new riding horses he'd bought for his place in the San Fernando Valley, and Wolfe of some land he'd just purchased in Santa Barbara.

When Strickland walked in, followed by Maggie and the ever-present Paulie Bianco, it was as if throngs of people had been waiting outside for him to lead them in at the head of a procession, and most of the booths and tables were suddenly filled.

After Strickland was seated, Paulie left to wait outside. Courtney, too, was there, and the group was complete. No one among them mentioned it, but they were all aware that their table, with five of the night's Academy Award nominees present, was the center of interest for the other people in the Polo Lounge.

Strickland ordered champagne around and offered a toast that not only would *The Amulet* win the night's awards but that they would all duplicate the feat the next year with the new film they were now meeting to discuss.

"Jim's brought along a couple of Xeroxes of the first draft of the script," he said. "He still wants to do some rewriting. But Halcie, Courtney" — he looked at each in turn — "I wanted you to see the script." He nodded toward King. "Jack's already read it."

Edgell handed Halcie and Courtney copies of the script.

Strickland, glancing around the table, talked of the new movie. It would be totally different from *The Amulet*. It would be a modern story of a younger woman, played by Courtney, and an older woman, played by Halcie, each of whom loses her husband. One of the switches in the story would be that the younger woman's husband dies, while the other woman's husband divorces her. Trying to comfort one another, each of the women comes to terms with her own life.

"Jim's managed to get a lot of wry humor as well as poignancy into the script," Strickland said. "The working title is *Misplaced Affection*."

"It's going to be a solid, quality film," King said quietly.

Strickland looked at Halcie. "Halcie, I know you'll need some time to read the script and make a decision. I don't want to put pressure on you, but Jim figures he'll have a shooting script finished in about two weeks. I'd like to be ready to go as soon as possible after that."

Halcie nodded. "I understand, Arthur."

"Good!" Strickland opened his attaché case, took out a folder, and handed it to Halcie. "I've had your contract prepared, so if your decision is affirmative you can have your agent call Herman."

Halcie nodded again, and Strickland, business concluded, settled back in his seat.

"Speaking of contracts," King said, "reminds me of a story that supposedly happened back when Harry Cohn was the head of Columbia Pictures. There was this bright young producer in New York who'd had a couple of hits on Broadway, and Cohn brought him out to Hollywood to offer him a producer's job at Columbia. They met in Cohn's office at the studio and everything went fine until Cohn brought out the contract. The young man looked it over, then handed it back, saying he knew it wasn't the contract given to other producers at Columbia. Cohn, indignant, demanded to know if the young man was suggesting that he, Harry Cohn, was a liar. The young man answered that if Cohn was saying that this was the studio's standard producer contract, well, yes, he *was* suggesting Cohn was a liar."

King paused, took a sip of champagne, and said, "Cohn looked at the young man for a moment, then leaned forward and, using the intercom on his desk, told his secretary: 'Now you can bring in the *real* contract.'"

They all laughed.

Ted Maury had been directing the live televised Academy Awards for three years. This night would be his fourth year, and the job never got any easier.

Now, at two on Tuesday afternoon of the night of the Oscar ceremonies, he sat in front of the bank of TV monitors in the trailer that served as the TV control booth. The trailer was located outside the Dorothy Chandler Pavilion, which was part of the Music Center of Los Angeles County, on Grand Street in downtown L. A.

Tonight, when the Awards took place, Maury in the trailer would have a better view of the interior of the Dorothy Chandler Pavilion than would any of the VIP's of the film world inside. In fact, with the thirteen cameras he could use – several of which were hand-held ones he could position wherever he chose – he could see on the monitors almost everywhere in the auditorium.

At the moment, he was rehearsing camera positions for shots of the stars sitting in the audience at the time their nominations were announced. For the purpose of camera rehearsal, oversized photographs of each had been placed in the seat already assigned to the star.

The seating for all the nominees was arranged so that actors and actresses were grouped together in one section, directors in another, writers in another. Maury checked the monitors as each camera in turn focused in on close-ups of the photographs of the faces, all full-frame, all on cue.

He lit a cigarette while one of the stage managers inside the auditorium set up the next shot. He lifted off his headset, took a sip of coffee from the thermos he'd filled earlier, and settled back in his chair.

So far so good, he thought, on this third and last day of rehearsals. There had been no real problems on the first day, Sunday. That was the day that most of the stars who would present the awards appeared to rehearse their lines from the TelePrompters.

In past years the biggest problem he'd had on the first day of rehearsal was that most of the big stars arrived with an entourage of secretary, manager, agent, press agent, hairdresser or bodyguard, and sometimes all six (everybody wanted to be in show business, he often thought). The problem then became how to separate the talent, for rehearsal, from the hangers-on. This year he solved the problem by having name cards put on the seats in order of the stars' appearance, which neatly relegated the entourage to the background.

Monday, which was dress rehearsal, had gone

off without any major hitches, and now he was almost through the last step, rehearsing camera positions.

Still, he reflected, the job never got any easier for the simple reason that, try as he might, he could never anticipate what might — and often did — go wrong when they were actually televising live to an audience of millions around the world.

The year before there was the incident of what he thought of as "the phantom troubadour." It happened about halfway through the ceremonies. The full orchestra was playing "The Magic of Love," one of the nominated songs; suddenly there was the sound of a male voice singing the lyrics "The magic of love is everywhere . . ." when there should have been no singer. The curtain was still down over the main stage where the on-air camera was focused.

Maury couldn't figure out what was happening. He started yelling over his microphone to all of his cameramen and to the stage managers. "Who's singing? For God's sake, find him and shut him up!"

The singing went on for more seconds, the curtain down over the main stage, until finally one of the cameramen reported: "We've spotted him. It's one of the stagehands. He must have had one too many. He's down in the orchestra pit. We're pulling him out."

Maury could see from a camera on one of the monitors that there was a scuffle going on in the orchestra pit; then he saw a man being hauled off backstage, and he was told: "We've removed him."

The orchestra continued to play, the curtain over the main stage went up, and the production number set to the music of "The Magic of Love" began, when again there was the sound of the male voice singing "I see your face in the stars above, it's the magic, the magic, the magic of love . . ." The singing continued throughout the production number, and it was only after the end of the show that Maury found out that the wrong person — one of the violinists — was grabbed the first time and hauled away, while "the phantom troubadour" went blissfully on singing!

It was a funny incident now, thinking back, but not so funny at the time.

The previous year there was the episode of the vanishing star.

At the Academy Awards ceremonies, most of the stars who would be presenters sat in the auditorium watching the show until just before time for them to appear onstage. Then they would go backstage and wait for their cue.

That year one of the biggest male stars in Hollywood, winner of the Oscar the year before who was to present the Oscar for Best Actress, went backstage — and disappeared.

The stage managers searched frantically for the actor before informing Maury he was nowhere to be found. Another actor in the audience was rushed backstage and brought on to make the presentation.

Again, it was only after the end of the show that Maury discovered a stage manager had eventually located the missing male star. He was in one of the dressing rooms, where he and a young female dancer on the show were making love.

Maury put on his headset for the next rehearsal shot, watching the monitor, and said into his microphone: "Camera one, Allie, get in just a shade closer on her face, please."

"Ted, I get in any closer, tonight the whole world'll see the zits on our star's face," the cameraman said jokingly, but moved the camera in tighter on the stand-in's face.

"Perfect shot," Maury said. Then he added, "And don't worry about the zits on our star's face — makeup'll take care of them. They'll look like beauty marks."

4

By late afternoon the whole front area outside the Dorothy Chandler Pavilion was jammed with movie fans who had gathered to cheer the celebrities arriving in their limousines for the Oscar ceremonies. As was true every year, some of those present in the crowd had been there since six-thirty in the morning to make sure they had a good spot from which to view the entrance to the auditorium. Some of the fans carried signs or photographs of their favorite stars, which they held in the air to attract the attention of those actors and actresses as they passed by. Police and security guard were there as well, although, as was true almost every year, the crowd was patient and orderly.

Maury sat in front of the bank of TV monitors in the control booth trailer and watched the scene outside through the three television cameras covering the entrance to the auditorium and occasionally panning across the

71

crowd. The cameras were taping the various celebrities as they arrived and as some of them were interviewed by Jerry Jekell, motion picture columnist for the *Hollywood Reporter*. Portions of the tape would be shown on the air at the opening of the Oscar telecast a couple of hours later.

Glancing back and forth among the three monitors, Maury's eye jump-cut from celebrity to celebrity and, now and then, to crowd shots on-camera: Kathleen Havens arriving; an interview with Gregory Peck; Bob Hope waving to the crowd; some of the crowd waving signs DIRTY HARRY!; Clint Eastwood waving to the crowd; Halcie Harper escorted by Jack King; the crowd shouting and cheering.

In the crowd a woman in the front row didn't notice she was being photographed as one of the cameras panned across the fans cheering Charlton Heston. The woman wouldn't have cared if she *had* noticed; she had other matters on her mind. She had been there, with some of the group, since six-thirty that morning. Unlike the others, however, she was not there to cheer but to kill — if she got the chance. She had been planning this day for months.

The cameras were recording a steady stream of limousines and celebrities arriving: Steven Spielberg Gene Hackman Jim Edgell Angie

Dickinson Frank Sinatra Oliver Stone Jane Fonda Kathleen Turner Michael J. Fox Debra Winger Anne Bancroft Mell Brooks Bette Midler Tom Cruise Diane Keaton Charles Bronson Faye Dunaway Tuesday Weld Arthur Strickland Sissy Spacek.

As Halcie leaned back in her seat in the auditorium, she thought briefly of the contrast between this Academy Awards ceremony and the first one she attended. That night, when she received her first Oscar, the crowd was not much larger than it would be a few years later at the MGM commissary at lunchtime. After the Awards, she and her husband, David, had gone partying. They had a little car, a roadster, and they got home very late. The next morning some people from the Academy came to get her Oscar to have it engraved — and she and David couldn't find it. David finally located it in the trunk of the roadster, where he had stuck it away before they went partying. Remembering the incident, she had to laugh to herself.

How little she had realized then that there would be a night like this at the Academy Awards, which would virtually equal the modern-day inauguration of a president or a royal coronation. If one wanted proof of the power of motion pictures, it seemed to her that, at least symbolically, this was it.

Maury had his eye on the clock as the hands moved second by second to air time. Then he said quietly into his microphone, using, as he always did, the old movie directors' cliché: "Lights, camera, action!"

The orchestra struck up an overture of the theme music from the five nominated films, the announcer came on, voice-over: "Live from the Dorothy Chandler Pavilion . . ." and the videotapes of the stars arriving went out on television around the world.

Halcie left her seat and hurried backstage as the curtains parted and the opening production number began, a surreal unfolding of the history of films — from the silents to stylized outer-space sequences — done in dance. She didn't much like following the opening production number, or what she had to do, but when they'd asked her she'd agreed.

She stood in the wings until the production number ended, the curtains on the main stage closed, and the announcer, voice-over, introduced her: "And now, the first lady of the American theater, Miss Halcyon Harper, who is also a past Oscar winner."

There was thunderous applause as she

walked to the microphone on the center-stage ramp, and she saw that the audience was giving her a standing ovation.

She stood in front of the microphone and smiled in acknowledgment of her reception and then, looking into the red light of the camera on the platform set up directly in front of the ramp, said:

"Thank you for your greeting. It's wonderful to be back in California to play a role in this most important evening for all of us who care about motion pictures, and I think that includes almost everyone who has ever attended a movie as well as those who have made movies.

"Now let me explain how our Oscar winners are selected. Who votes on these Academy Awards of merit? Who nominates them? And here's the answer. All eligible Academy members are asked to vote for nominations for the Best Picture of the Year. The other nominations are made by members of Academy branches, specialists in their fields. Actors nominate actors, film editors nominate film editors, and so on.

"Finally, Academy members vote by secret ballot for all the awards of merit and send their ballots directly to the Academy's independent accountants, Price, Waterhouse and Company, for tabulation.

"The results are known only to Price, Waterhouse, and representatives of that firm will hand the sealed envelopes containing the winners' names to the presenters during this show.

"Bearing the first envelope to present the first Oscar are two of this year's nominees, Carla Alberti and the distinguished president of the Screen Actors Guild, Lewis Worth."

Halcie hurried off stage, thinking bemusedly that what she had just done must be somewhat equivalent to trying to entertain an audience by reading names from a telephone directory.

Jim Edgell would have liked to be Courtney Ware's escort for the Awards, but Arthur Strickland had decreed other arrangements for those connected with *The Amulet*. And, since the evening was after all as much a business gathering as it was a social one, no one, including Edgell, could really object.

That was why Jack King and Halcie Harper were together, Eddie McCoy again accompanied Courtney, and Edgell had been asked to take a young actress, Zoe Rushell, who had already been picked by Strickland for a role in his next picture, *Misplaced Affection*. Strickland explained that it would be good exposure for the young actress to be seen at the Awards with a nominee for the screenplay Oscar. Strickland himself brought Maggie Geneen. Separated from his wife as he was, there could be no gossip about having invited his assistant.

Edgell liked Zoe well enough. She was young, slim, very pretty, her hair coal black, fringe-cut, her eyes deep blue, and there was a sweetness about her barely suppressed excitement at attending the Academy Awards. The trouble was that all through the ceremonies he kept wishing that he was with Courtney, who sat in the row of seats just ahead of him.

Onstage there was a fashion show production number of costumes from the films that were nominated for Best Costume Design. *The Amulet* had not received a nomination in that category.

Courtney, in the audience, turned her attention from the stage to observe what she thought of as the pantomime shadow play being enacted simultaneously in the front rows of seats in the auditorium. From time to time, all around her, silent figures slipped in from the sides of the auditorium and sat down wherever a star going backstage left a seat empty. When the star returned, the shadowy figure quickly moved out of the seat.

At first when she'd noticed the eerie figures gliding in and out of the rows of seats, she thought they were gate-crashers trying to grab a reserved seat for themselves. But then, in one of the breaks in the show while a commercial was being televised, Eddie explained to her that the shadowy figures had been hired for the job of filling seats when the stars had to leave briefly. Otherwise, when the camera cut to shots of the audience, TV viewers would see empty seats here and there and think that some star or other hadn't shown up or had left during the ceremonies. It was, Courtney thought, another example, although harmless enough, of the make-believe of Movieland.

There were elaborate production numbers built around the five songs nominated for an Oscar.

For the title song from *The Amulet,* the curtain opened on a stage filled with dancers, male and female, wearing Indian costumes from the film. The faces of the dancers were painted with colorful ritual markings — the whole presentation similar to a scene in the film — while across the back of the stage were giant blowups of the paintings used in the movie. In the center of the dancers, on a raised platform, stood one of country music's leading female vocalists, Young Rose Hightree, herself part Indian, who sang the lyrics.

When the number ended, King leaned over to Halcie and said in a loud whisper: *"That ought to finally satisfy Marlon Brando."*

There was laughter from those near enough to overhear the remark and who remembered the incident some years earlier when Brando, to dramatize the plight of the forgotten Indian peoples, sent a young Indian woman to pick up the Oscar he had won.

Edgell received the award for the Best Original Screenplay and said he wished he'd hired a writer to put into words an acceptance speech more original than the only one he could think of, which was simply "Thank you."

Halcie was honestly embarrassed when, after she accepted the award for Best Supporting Actress, she was given a second standing ovation.

King was – unusual for him – serious as he was presented with the Oscar for Best Director, saying he was indeed honored to be sharing the award with such giant directing talents as Frank Capra, John Ford, John Huston, Billy Wilder, Alfred Hitchcock, George Stevens, Howard Hawks, Orson Welles and, of course, D.W. Griffith, among others.

Long-Legged Lady won the award for Best Original Song, from the film *Black and Blues*.

Courtney had tears in her eyes as she held up

her Oscar for Best Actress and thanked the members of the Academy who had voted for her and all the people who had worked on *The Amulet*.

Ted Maury began to relax. The show was almost over and nothing terrible had happened. They were running clips now from the five films that were nominated for Best Picture. And then there would be the final award.

In the auditorium the film clips appeared on the giant screen above the main stage:

Fire Zone! was a Vietnam war movie in which only American soldiers were shown fighting an unseen enemy, which had the advantage of avoiding showing bloodshed and, some critics had writen, was subtly symbolic.

Chinese Takeout was a hip Manhattan film about an intellectual nebbish who gets involved with a tall, gorgeous lingerie model and sets out to educate her about the finer things in life, only to find in the end that she has a Ph.D., while he failed to graduate from Brooklyn's Erasmus Hall High School.

Home Run! was about a major league baseball pitcher who loses his pitching arm in an automobile accident, then learns to pitch all over again with his other arm and returns to baseball to lead his team to a World Series championship.

Staying Home was a film about four generations of both a white family and a black family in the South and the births, marriages, successes, failures, and deaths in the two families as their town and the nation change about them.

The final film clip was of *The Amulet*.

"And the winner is . . ." Another legendary screen actress, Joyce Kimbro, who had been invited to present the award for Best Motion Picture, opened the envelope. ". . . *The Amulet*, produced by Arthur G. Strickland Productions, Producer: Arthur G. Strickland."

Strickland kissed Miss Kimbro on the cheek as he accepted his Oscar. Before he could turn to the microphone to make his speech, Joan Strickland had joined him onstage. He didn't even know she was in the auditorium. She had been invited by Marty Cowell, and when *The Amulet* was announced as Best Picture she had, on impulse, simply gone up to the stage. She was damned if after all she had gone through with Strickland and the money she'd put into the production, she wasn't at least going to be standing beside him when he accepted the award.

There was a moment of awkward hesitation onstage; then Strickland faced the camera and said what a great honor it was to receive the

81

Oscar. He thanked all the people who had worked on the film, ending with a nod toward Joan, saying, "Including this lady, Joan Strickland."

Maury lit a cigarette as the show went to a series of commercials. In the auditorium, the stage filled with the performers, presenters, and Oscar winners who'd appeared earlier, as they took places for the last number, the grand finale.

The commercials ended and on-screen appeared a panoramic shot of the stage with everyone lined up in rows, swaying back and forth in rhythm as the orchestra played the song "Hollywood."

Maury cut back and forth between cameras to get a closer pan shot of various individuals onstage.

"Stand by to roll credits," he said into his microphone.

Camera 3, mounted on the platform in front of the ramp center-stage, was making a slow pan across the crowd onstage, and Maury had a hand out to cut to a wide shot over which the credits would roll, when suddenly someone onstage pitched forward and landed face down.

For an instant he couldn't see who had fallen or what was happening.

In the next instant the number 3 cameraman,

out of his conditioned reflex to get a shot of what was happening, zoomed in for a close-up on the prone figure.

On-screen and televised live over the air to an audience of over one billion viewers was the close-up picture of Arthur Strickland lying unmoving, a knife in his back, the blade buried deep between his shoulder blades. His Oscar lay beside him.

Maury was aware of the shocked confusion onstage and in the audience, and even in the orchestra, where some of the musicians had stopped playing while others kept on, the music discordant. He could see that some of the people onstage were milling around where Strickland lay, and a man was bent over the body. He also knew that someone on that stage had stuck the knife into Strickland. The police would want to know who. He realized it would be important to tape as much of the scene as possible.

At the moment only the on-air camera was being taped, by the network's Central Control in Burbank, through which everything televised in the auditorium was transmitted to the nation and to the world.

The technical director, sitting next to Maury in the trailer, was in constant contact with Central Control, and now Maury said quickly to him: "Tell Control to roll separate tapes on cameras one, four, and eight." He then gave orders over his microphone to the three cameras in the auditorium to get as many shots as possible, from different angles, of all the people onstage.

Only seconds had passed since camera 3 had zoomed in for a close-up of Strickland. On-screen now, the man who had bent over him stood up – Maury recognized him as Jack King – and shook his head.

Arthur Strickland was dead.

The technical director said, "Central Control thinks this is a big news story; they want us to keep televising live. They're going to do a voice-over report from the newsroom."

Maury nodded. Then he said to the assistant director, sitting behind him in the trailer, "Call nine-one-one. Tell them we've got a murder here – in case they don't already know it."

5

Lieutenant John Staver, LAPD, shouldered his way though the mass of people blocking the entrance to the Dorothy Chandler Pavilion. Ahead of him three uniformed cops tried to clear a path, and he was followed by two members of the Los Angeles Homicide Task Force, the special unit he commanded. The murder of Arthur Strickland would be their case to investigate.

Once inside, Staver reflected briefly that the setting was not the usual murder scene. Instead of the squalid surroundings in which police first came upon most dead bodies, here all was glittering chandeliers and plush carpeting and drapes, not unlike a grand ball with the men dressed in dinner jackets, the women in expensive gowns. More than half of the people who had been in the audience had left their seats but remained lingering at the rear of the auditorium and the entranceway, as if they wanted to put some distance between themselves and the presence of the corpse but were held to the scene by curiosity.

Arthur Strickland's body lay on the stage. A dozen uniformed cops had cleared a space around the body. Five plainclothes detectives from the Homicide Task Force had already begun interrogating possible witnesses. Police photographers were shooting pictures of the corpse, while a large group of press photographers were shooting pictures of the police photographers.

Staver realized that of course there were plenty of press photographers on hand since they were already in the auditorium to take pictures of the Oscar winners.

The uniformed cops and the Homicide Task Force plainsclothesmen had been directed to the scene by this dispatcher as soon as the call to 911 came in. Staver and the two members of his unit were late in arriving because they had been witnesses in federal court that afternoon and afterward had gone for Mexican food on Brooklyn Avenue. Staver had just started his meal when he felt the beeper signal he wore pulsating against his hip. In federal court so many of the people involved in the proceedings — lawyers, cops, and businessmen — wore pagers that they were requested to turn the sound off. At the restaurant Staver still had the sound turned off. He'd gone to a phone, called the precinct, and was told of the murder at the Academy Awards.

When Staver reached the auditorium, he went first to take a look at the body. The precinct dispatcher had told him the victim was an Arthur Strickland, a movie producer. Staver was not familiar with the name, but he noticed the golden Oscar lying next to the body. The poor bastard must have just won an Academy Award.

Staver next examined the knife protruding from the back of the body. It looked to him like a carving knife with, from what he could see of it, a thick blade. There was very little blood.

He looked up as Sergeant Frank Murch, of the task force, approached.

"You're gonna love this case, Lieutenant," Murch said.

"How's that?"

Murch waved a hand in the air. "He's knifed right here on the stage and falls over with everybody in the place watching and the TV cameras going, too, but so far, since he got it in the back, we can't find anyone that saw who did it."

Staver frowned. "None of the people on the stage around him, behind him, saw anything?"

"They say they didn't," Murch said, "the ones we've questioned. Some of the people who were on the stage had disappeared by the time we got here. We'll have to track them down later. The ones we've talked to" — he shrugged — "I guess they were too busy smiling at the camera."

Staver nodded. He was looking around at the people who were still onstage. He was, he thought, seeing more movie stars in person at one time than he had seen before in his entire lifetime in Los Angeles.

He looked back at Sergeant Murch. "Somebody must have a list of all the people who were onstage tonight. We have to get a copy of it, make sure we question everyone."

Murch nodded.

"Another thing," Staver said. "Find the head of the security guards working tonight. Check if any of the guards reported any incidents of a person or persons crashing the ceremonies."

They were interrupted when a man who had a headset hanging around his neck walked over and said to Staver: "One of the policemen pointed you out as the officer in charge."

"I am. I'm Lieutenant Staver."

"I'm a stage manager," the man said. "My boss, the director — the TV director, Ted Maury — wanted me to tell you he's been making tape recordings of the stage, the people onstage, since the moment he saw Strickland fall. He thought you might like to see the tapes."

"I would," Staver said. "Where is he?"

"He probably won't be able to show you the tapes until tomorrow. But you can talk to him now." He pointed offstage. "He's still working in the trailer outside there."

Staver felt suddenly uncomfortable. "You mean he's still taping what's going on here?" He looked around for the first time at the TV cameras, then spotted a large monitor at the side of the stage. The men from the coroner's office arrived to remove the body to the morgue, and on the screen of the monitor Staver could see them and the body and, in the background, himself, Murch, and the stage manager.

The stage manager, answering Staver's question, said, "There's some tape being made, yeah. We're still televising live."

Staver was astonished. "Do I understand correctly that we're being televised live everywhere at this very moment?"

"Right." The stage manager nodded. "Network thought it was a big enough story to keep it on the air. But the TV audience can't hear anything being said here. The mikes in here are off; they're doing a voice-over report from Central Control's studio in Burbank."

"We can be thankful for that, at least," Staver said, but he felt acutely uncomfortable. He wanted the show off. He looked at Sergeant Murch and jerked a thumb toward the men from the coroner's office. "Tell them to get moving with that body. And as fast as the people on the stage have been questioned, get them out of here, too."

He had picked up a phrase watching *The Tonight Show* with Johnny Carson: He noticed that between the show and the commercials viewers were informed the show would continue by the words on the screen: "More To Come." The phrase had stuck in his mind because it reminded him it was always that way during the stages of an investigation. Now as he went to find Ted Maury, he thought: More To Come.

From the moment Eddie McCoy realized Arthur Strickland was dead, he knew he still had a job to do, murder or no murder. This was, after all, Academy Awards night. Press photographers from all over the world were there to take pictures of the winners, and he was press agent for a movie that had won five Oscars. He wasn't about to let a murder, even

Arthur Strickland's murder, completely upstage his Academy Award winners. The photographers might have enough pictures of the late Arthur G. Strickland, but he had four other winners whose pictures he wanted in the next day's papers.

The trouble was, it wasn't easy to round up Jack King, Courtney Ware, Jim Edgell, and Halcie Harper in all the confusion in the auditorium, especially after the police arrived and started their questioning. He himself had been backstage at the time of the grand finale, for the very purpose of getting them all together for the photo session in the pressroom. He had heard the orchestra begin to play "Hollywood" and then the eerie way the music changed, and he knew something was wrong. Then he heard a babble of sounds, stifled cries, voices, from the stage and from the audience. Suddenly people were rushing past him from the direction of the stage. He tried to find out what had happened; one of the performers, a young girl, told him in a frightened voice: "Somebody's dead. They said somebody's dead onstage," and hurried away.

He went out onstage. Some people were moving around aimlessly, some were standing still, others were leaving. He couldn't see anybody he knew. He kept moving through the crowd until he spotted Jim Edgell and hurried over to him.

Edgell looked white-faced, stunned.

Eddie grabbed him by the arm and asked, "What the hell's going on, Jim?"

Edgell looked at him. "It's Arthur. Arthur's dead. Somebody stabbed him."

Edgell pulled away, and Eddie pushed through the crowd until he was close enough to see for himself.

None of it could be real, Eddie thought, glancing out at the filled auditorium, at the TV cameras focused on the stage, looking around at the stage itself where stood some of the most famous celebrities in the world.

And then he realized he still had a job to do that night, and he needed to get Courtney, Halcie, King, and Edgell together.

Before he could look for them, however, Didi Jones came rushing toward him. The columnist had been in the audience and had come up onstage, knowing she had a hot story on her hands.

Eddie wished there was a way to escape, but that was impossible to do without deliberately ignoring her, and he couldn't risk that. He had to stand there and submit to her questions.

No, he didn't know who would have wanted Arthur dead.

No, he didn't know of any enemies Arthur might have had.

No, he hadn't noticed that Arthur had been worried or upset any time in the recent past.

She finally left, and by then the police were there, asking questions of everyone onstage.

The detective who interrogated Eddie wanted to see some identification, wrote down his name, address, and phone number. He asked where Eddie had been when the victim was stabbed, if he had seen who might have done the stabbing, if he knew the victim personally. The final question was if Eddie knew of anyone who might have committed the murder.

When the detective finished with him, Eddie saw that Halcie and King were also being questioned. He couldn't spot Courtney anywhere, and he discovered that Edgell was nowhere to be seen, either. He wondered if they'd left the auditorium. He hoped they hadn't.

He waited and then rounded up Halcie and King after they concluded their talks with the police. Edgell came back to the stage at the same time. He said he'd gone down into the audience to look for Zoe. She had left, apparently frightened by the events that had taken place, as others in the audience had. And, he said wryly, he guessed she had taken the limousine that had brought them, leaving him stranded, without a ride home.

Eddie assured Edgell they'd work that out later. For now, Eddie explained, he wanted the three of them to go to the pressroom with him to have their pictures taken with their Oscars. It was important for all of them, and he wanted Courtney to be there, too, if she hadn't left.

One of the detectives came over to question Edgell, and Eddie left the three of them and went to look for Courtney. More police had arrived, and Eddie saw that Arthur's body was being removed.

And then he saw Courtney as he was making a slow circle around the stage. She was surrounded by a group of eight or nine people, and Eddie went over. The people in the group were listening as Courtney was talking with another of the detectives, who was asking her the same series of questions Eddie himself had answered earlier. When the detective had finished and gone in search of other possible witnesses, a couple of the people standing near Courtney asked her for her autograph.

Eddie saw that she was surprised by the requests at such an inappropriate time, but she signed her name for those who had asked her. He moved in before more people might approach her, took her by the arm, and led her away.

She gave him a smile. "Oh, Lord, Eddie, what a — a craziness! People asking me for my autograph right in the middle of a police investigation of a murder!"

He patted her hand. "It's the price of fame, baby," he said. "Don't knock it."

They were all subdued, Courtney, Halcie, Jack King, and Edgell, as Eddie escorted them up to the seventh floor of the pavilion. On this one night of the annual Academy Awards the rooms on the seventh floor, which were normally rehearsal rooms for productions staged at the pavilion, were transformed into various quarters for the media. One was an interview room for the reporters, one a photo room for the still photographers, one a room for radio interviews, one a room where the news television cameras were set up for TV interviews. Security guards, hired by the Academy of Motion Picture Arts and Sciences, were everywhere to keep out intruders.

There were other celebrities present, other Oscar winners of the night, and presenters of the Awards. Most of the attention of the press photographers, press interviewers, and radio and television people was centered on Courtney and Halcie. King did several press interviews, had his photograph taken, and did some radio interviews. Edgell had his photograph taken and was interviewed on radio.

When it was over and they were on their way down from the seventh floor, Eddie reminded them that there was still the Academy's Governor's Ball at the Beverly Hilton Hotel that night and, later, the party Milton Golub gave at the Bistro Restaurant each year after the Awards.

Halcie shook her head. "I'm sorry, Eddie. There's been more than enough excitement for one night. I'm exhausted. I'm going home."

King didn't want to attend either event. He expressed what most of them felt: Everybody everywhere would be wanting to gossip about Arthur's murder, and he didn't want to talk about it or hear about it this soon after.

Eddie understood; he felt that way himself. But he said he thought someone connected with *The Amulet* should make at least a brief appearance at the Governor's Ball. He talked Courtney into going with him, even though she really wanted to go home; after all, he pointed out, she was the actress of the year.

At any other time Edgell would have gone along simply because of Courtney, but after King offered him a ride in the limousine he was sharing with Halcie, he decided to pass up both affairs, too.

The group had to wait until the limousines came to pick them up in front of the pavilion. Halcie glanced around at the others. It was the first time it had occurred to her that one of them might be the murderer of Arthur Strickland.

"Years ago," Jack King said, leaning back in the booth across the table from Edgell, "I was in Ben Hecht's office in the Writers Building at Metro. Stuck on the wall right in front of his typewriter — as if to inspire him to greater creative heights — was this giant blowup of a single typed line of shooting script: CUT TO CHASE."

King grinned. Edgell laughed.

King took a drink of scotch and unwrapped a fresh cigar.

The two of them were in a bar near Los Angeles International Airport, just off Sepulveda Boulevard.

They'd dropped Halcie off at Laura Harrow's house, and Edgell had accepted when King asked him if he'd like to stop somewhere and have a few drinks. King had the driver take them to the bar near the airport and told the driver to come back for them a couple of hours later.

King explained to Edgell that he'd discovered the bar — Mickey's, it was called — a long time ago when he was directing a film on location at the airport. There was nothing special about the place, just a friendly hangout for the people who lived and worked in the neighborhood. Over the years King had come back when he wanted to do some quiet drinking away from the usual Hollywood spots, where he was known and knew everybody. At Mickey's, even though the regulars knew who he was, they paid no more attention to him than if he was just another customer from the neighborhood.

Edgell thought he could understand why King would like the place. It shared certain characteristics with all good drinking bars: the all-wood interior — floor, chairs, tables, booths, the wood paneling framing the glass mirror behind the bar, with the multiple rows of bottles reflected in the mirror. There was, too, that good drinking bar-smell; Edgell thought of it as the smell of malt and hops and astringent spirits, gin, scotch, bourbon, ingrained in the wood of the bar, the floor, the tables from countless spilled drinks. The atmosphere was conducive to good drinking, and the look and smell had a lot to do with it, as it must have had in the best pubs and alehouses of a century earlier, and even the saloons of the Old West.

There was a double row of drinkers standing at the bar across from the booth where Edgell and King sat, and there was a large-screen television set above the bar with the picture on but the sound off. The owner, Mickey Donnelly, served as his own bartender.

When King and Edgell had ordered their drinks — a full quart of Chivas Regal and a pitcher of water for King, and for Edgell, who'd ordered beer, a dozen bottles in a bucket of ice brought by Mickey — they talked.

Or rather King talked.

Edgell was reminded of one of his favorite lines from Dashiell Hammett's *The Maltese Falcon* when the fat man, Caspar Gutman, says to Sam Spade: "Now, sir, we'll talk, if you like. And I'll tell you right out that I'm a man who likes talking to a man who likes to talk." At that moment, Edgell thought, you could say he was a man who liked to listen to a man, if it was Jack King, who liked to talk.

King talked about his early days in Hollywood. He got his first job in the movies when he wrote a script, a Western, and it was bought by a producer at the old Republic Studios.

The film was shot out in the desert, in one of the deserted ghost towns, and made use of the setting as it existed. The story was simple: The heroine was kidnapped by a gang of bad guys and taken out to the desert, while the hero pursued them, fought a gun battle, killed all the bad guys, and rescued her.

King laughed. "Talk about low-budget Westerns — this was a no-budget Western."

He shook his head as he recalled that money on the picture was so tight that they could only scrape together enough to transport two horses out to the desert. The director would film two men riding the two horses, then cut, put two other men in the saddles and film them, cut, and so on until he had achieved the effect of the gang riding along two by two behind each other.

After that first sale, King said, he wrote three more scripts, but nobody would buy them. To earn money, he worked for the studio as a driver, a horse wrangler, and a prop man, writing in between. He wrote twenty-one screenplays and was never able to sell any of them.

About that time, there was a party one night up in the Hollywood Hills given by one of the art directors at the studio. King was invited. "In those days movie people went to parties somewhere almost every night," he explained. "Wherever there was booze."

He didn't know many people at the party,

and one of them he didn't know was a man who came over and started talking to him toward the end of the evening. Somebody at the party had told the man that King was a scriptwriter.

King took a drink of scotch. "This guy asked me a lot of questions about how I went about writing screenplays. Guy looked like a truck-driver — chunky, bushy-haired, talked tough."

He was flattered, he said, didn't tell the man he'd only sold one script, and tried to give him some tips on how to write screenplays as if he himself really knew.

He smiled, looking at Edgell. "This guy listened most respectfully until I finished and thanked me. Then the guy tells me he's tried writing screenplays but they just didn't work. I sympathize with him. He says — listen to this — he says, 'I've been a screenwriter at almost every studio in Hollywood and I washed out.' The guy looks like he can't believe it. He says, 'I started out earning two hundred and fifty dollars a week and wound up getting paid twelve hundred dollars a week, and I washed out every time. But every time I was out at one studio, a novel of mine would come out and another studio would hire me at more money.' "

King took a drink of scotch and said, "The guy shakes my hand, and before I can ask any questions, he's left the party. So I rush over to my host to find out who the guy was, and I'm floored when I find out I'd been talking to James M. Cain.

"That night, at home after the party, I did a lot of thinking. I was mesmerized when I read Cain's *The Postman Always Rings Twice, Double Indemnity, Mildred Pierce,* and *Serenade.* Here was the writer who practically invented a new dialogue, speech that was perfect for the screen, and wrote tight, quick-cut plots made for the movies. If he didn't think he could make it as a screenwriter, I didn't see any future for myself."

The next day, King said, he went into the studio, found the producer who filmed his first script, and told him he had an idea for a movie but thought somebody else should write the script and he'd direct. Everything connected with the business was a lot more casual in those days, King explained to Edgell.

The producer liked King's movie idea, got a scriptwriter, and gave King the chance to direct.

The film was another low-budget Western, the story of a small town that has to defend itself when a gang of bad guys rides in to shoot it up. The town's minister gathers all the townspeople inside the church to get them off the street and protect them, preaching nonviolence. The gang rides in, the minister goes out and tells them the town wants no trouble, that the gang can take anything they want and ride on out and there'll be no shooting. Of course, what happens is that the gang sacks the houses and buildings, and then attacks the church and the people in it. And of course, the townspeople, with the minister leading them, finally use their guns and wipe out the gang down to the last man. The title of the film was *The Gunsmen.*

The film made some money, and King went on to direct a dozen more Westerns. In time he was given more important movies to direct and won his first Oscar in 1960.

"The Stand-In," Edgell said. "It's my favorite film about Hollywood."

King nodded. *"The Stand-In."* He lit another cigar and filled his glass. Some of the scotch and water sloshed over onto the table, Edgell noticed, thinking King was feeling his drinks. He himself had what he though of as a buzz-on from all the beer he'd drunk.

"Yeah, *The Stand-In* was a good film," King said. He lifted his glass, holding it carefully, and took a drink.

"You know what makes a good film, Writer?" King always called Edgell "Writer" instead of by name, a way he had of showing he liked him. "Mastery of craft is what makes a good film. Probably true of any product made, as they say, for mass consumption. Certainly true of films. You need craftsmen, writers, actors, technicians, who know their craft. It's a craft form. All that *critique* crap about movies being an art form" — he waved a hand in the air.

"I can see that," Edgell nodded.

King nodded, too, and suddenly changed the subject. "You ever been married?"

"No. No, I never have."

"I thought not," King said. "I have. Five times. Five times married, five times divorced. And you know something? I loved every one of them when we got married, I love every one of them still." He paused and then said. "You and Courtney, she been giving you a hard time lately?"

Edgell wasn't really surprised that King didn't miss much of what went on around him. He said, "She says she's been busy."

King nodded slowly. "Women. I'll tell you, Writer, the secret to falling in love with them is" — he took a puff on his cigar and blew out the smoke — "not to get emotionally involved."

Edgell laughed out loud. King grinned.

They both drank and King set his empty

glass down on the table. "Ready to call it a night?"

"Ready."

King pushed himself halfway up from the seat, paused there as he glanced at the television set behind the bar, and said, "Banquo's ghost has returned to haunt us all."

Edgell saw the TV set, too: It must have been turned to a news show, and on-screen were pictures of Arthur Strickland lying onstage at the Academy Awards, the knife sticking in his back.

And King's words were true, Edgell thought, his eyes on the TV screen: Shakespeare, bringing onstage the ghost of the murdered Banquo in *Macbeth*, was ahead of his time. Now TV, with film and videotape, ceaselessly summoned up the ghostly memories of the tragedies of today's times, frequently with instant recall.

Edgell looked around the room. Nobody else was looking at the television set.

On their way out of the bar, King, in a remark again reflecting his acerbic view of the absurdities of life, said, "You have to admit, Writer, between Arthur's winning an Oscar and getting stabbed in the back, tonight's probably the first time *every* member of the Academy's ever agreed on one thing: Arthur Strickland finally got what he deserved."

6

Lieutenant Staver had called a meeting of his Homicide Task Force for 7:30 A.M., and was himself a quarter of an hour late getting to the precinct.

The heavy rain had delayed him on the drive from his apartment on Laurel Avenue, just off Fountain in West Hollywood, to the Central Division precinct where the special unit had improvised quarters, with a small squad room and a private office, not much larger than a closet, for Staver.

The other six members of the team were waiting in the squad room: Frank Murch, Will Tobin, Andy Tomasini, Peter Ardis, Morrie Fried, and Ed Cooney, drinking coffee and drying out from the rain. Staver gave them a wave of the hand and went into his office.

He hung up his wet slicker in the closet and took the lid off the cup of coffee he'd picked up at the coffee shop next door. He lit a cigarette, drank some coffee, and walked over to the window.

Outside, the rain was beating down. The storm must have blown in sometime during the early hours of the morning, a spring storm with hard, steady rain and gusting winds. From the look of the black sky and the pouring rain collecting ankle-high in the gutters of the street, Staver figured they were in for an all-day downpour.

He went to the door of his office and called in the detectives, who were still drinking coffee in the squad room. When they had all taken places around his desk, he said, "No need to tell you, I'm sure, that the Strickland murder is top priority. There's going to be a lot of heat coming down from all sides on this one. The mayor, the commissioner, the chief, the media, the public are going to be dogging us every step of the way. We're all going to feel it."

He was reminding them that Los Angeles, despite all its other commerce, was still, above all, a company town, and that company was the motion picture industry. The Hollywood of films gave L. A. its world image. There would be no letup from the media or from any other quarter until the Strickland murder was solved.

Staver glanced down at the papers on his desk. The night before, after the team left the

Dorothy Chandler Pavilion, all of the detectives typed up interrogation reports on the people they had questioned onstage at the auditorium. In addition, Staver had picked up a copy of a list of the people who were a part of the show and were thought to be onstage during the finale.

Before he checked out of the precinct the night before, he read over the reports and the list. Some of the people who had been thought to be onstage were not among those who had been interrogated; either they had not appeared onstage at the end of the show or they had left before the police arrived. They would have to be found and questioned as soon as possible. Also, among the interrogation reports were statements taken from people who presumably were not supposed to be onstage; some of them said they had come up from the audience or from backstage after the finale but before the police got to the auditorium. They, too, would have to be requestioned more carefully.

Staver had made Xeroxes of the list, with circles drawn around the names of those who had not been questioned, and he passed them around to the six detectives.

"Frank'll coordinate the assignment," Staver said, nodding toward Sergeant Murch. "You'll work through him." He lit a cigarette. "That's the bad news. The good news is that I have an appointment shortly in Burbank with the TV people to look at the videotapes they made last night. With luck they just might show us who the killer was. And the security people working the Awards last night reported there were two separate incidents of individuals trying to crash the ceremonies. One was a man, one a woman. The chief of security and two of his men who ejected the crashers will be in Burbank, too, to look at the tapes." He looked around the room. "Any questions?" When there were none, he said, "Okay, let's move."

Alone again, Staver started reading through the interrogation reports, noting down on a separate paper the names of all those who appeared to be closely associated with Arthur Strickland. They would reasonably be the most likely suspects in the case. If the videotapes failed to ID the killer, these were the possible suspects he wanted to question personally.

He had just finished reading through the last of the reports when his phone rang. It was the desk sergeant out front.

"Lieutenant, you have a visitor. I think you'd better come out, sir."

Before Staver could ask a question, the desk sergeant had disconnected.

The Homicide Task Force offices were in the

back of the building on the first floor. When Staver got to the booking desk in the front, there was a large circle of male and female officers gathered. He edged his way through the group, saying, "Pardon me, excuse me," until he saw the woman standing in the midst of the crowd. He recognized her immediately as Halcie Harper, the actress. She was signing autographs. He had seen her the night before at the auditorium and had read her statement in one of the interrogation reports, but he had not spoken with her at the Dorothy Chandler Pavilion. The police officers who had collected around her began to scatter when they noticed him. He said to her, "I'm Lieutenant Staver, ma'am. You wanted to see me."

"Oh, yes, Lieutenant," Halcie said, finishing off the autograph she was signing and handing it to one of the female officers. "Last night at the Oscars, I asked one of the detectives who was in charge of the investigation of Arthur Strickland's murder. He gave me your name and told me where I'd find you. May I speak with you?"

"Yes, sure."

Staver led her back to his office. She sat in a chair in front of his desk, placing her wet raincoat over the arm of another chair and leaning her umbrella against the side of his desk.

"Now what can I do for you, Miss Harper?" Staver asked.

Halcie shook her head. "It's such a terrible thing, Arthur Strickland's death. I don't suppose you know yet who did it?"

"No. No, we don't."

Halcie sighed. "I was afraid of that. But I do have some information I thought you ought to know about. Did you know that just recently Arthur had been receiving anonymous death threats?"

Staver was startled. "No, I didn't know that."

Halcie nodded. "Not many people did know, I understand. But I was told he went to the police about them and that they didn't really take them too seriously. Anyhow, now, since you're in charge of the investigation of his murder, I thought you should know."

"You're right," Staver said. "The notes — do you know where they are now?"

"At his house, I would imagine. I really don't know. I'm sure you could check."

"We'll check," Staver said. "Did you ever see the notes?"

"No. I was told about them."

"And who told you, Strickland himself?"

Halcie was silent for a moment before she asked, "Do I have to answer that? I mean, it

111

was just something somebody, a friend, told me."

"I think it would be helpful if you told me," Staver said gently.

"It was Jack King, the director," she said slowly. "He's a friend — was a friend — of Arthur's. He's a friend of mine. I don't think it was any great secret, about the anonymous notes, but Arthur just didn't want a lot of people gossiping."

"Did he take the threats seriously, Strickland? Do you know?"

"I was told," Halcie said, again slowly, "that he hired a bodyguard. Arthur apparently didn't want people to know about *that*, either. He told everybody the bodyguard, Paulie Bianco, was his chauffeur. Or so I was told."

Staver was silent for a moment, quickly turning over the papers on his desk until he found the one he wanted.

He looked up at Halcie. "Paulie Bianco. One of my men questioned him last night. He was among those onstage when we arrived. He said he was backstage at the time Strickland was killed. Any idea why he'd be there, backstage?"

"I really don't know." Halcie shook her head. "I would suppose, though, that after Arthur won an Oscar, if his chauffeur went backstage and told them Arthur wanted him there, they'd let him stay. The security people at the auditorium should be able to answer that for you."

Staver made a note on the report and pushed back his chair. "You've been a big help, Miss Harper. I appreciate your coming to see me."

Halcie sat still in the chair. "Tell me, Lieutenant Staver, with all those TV cameras on, don't you have any leads at all?"

He thought for a moment and then decided to tell her. "As a matter of fact I'm going out to Burbank right now to meet with Ted Maury, the TV director, to take a look at the tapes they made last night."

"Good!" Halcie placed both hands down hard on the arms of her chair. "And you know what? I think you should let me be there, too."

"Wait! Hold on a moment!" Staver had raised a hand in the air.

Halcie kept talking fast. "You're going to need someone present who can tell you who all the different people are on the stage, particularly the people who were a close part of Arthur's life. The TV director will know some of them. I know all of them. I really think you should let me be there."

"Well . . ." Staver decided it would make sense and probably save time to have her there, ". . . all right. Okay."

Halcie was pleased and excited. She had a car

waiting for her outside. Staver would go in one of the precinct's unmarked cars. After he told her where to meet him in Burbank, she left ahead of him. He put on his rain slicker, thinking how strange life was, that he should be talking to Halcie Harper, an actress — no, a personality, whose name he had known since as far back as he could remember.

Leaving the station house, he was struck by another thought: The last time he saw Halcie Harper perform was in a movie on TV when she played the role of the busybody Miss Marple, in an Agatha Christie story, who solved the murder for the police. He hoped that she wasn't confusing real life with a movie role. Or that he wasn't.

Halcie settled into her seat in the TV studio screening room, thinking that the room was almost exactly like the one at the Centurion Studios where she had sometimes stopped in to view the daily rushes during the filming of *The Amulet*. There were the same kind of theater seats sloping down from the rear of the room, the same slot for the projectionist back there in the booth, the same blank white screen centered in front of the rows of seats.

She sat alone in the first row. Staver and the three security men from the Dorothy Chandler

Pavilion sat together in the row behind her, and Ted Maury moved around from seat to seat, his voice coming out of the darkness from one direction or another when the lights went out and scenes on the videotape began to appear on-screen.

"These are the opening shots of the grand finale number," Maury's disembodied voice announced.

There was a panoramic shot of the stage with the performers, presenters, and Oscar winners lined up in rows, swaying back and forth in rhythm as the orchestra played the song "Hollywood."

Halcie looked first for − and spotted − herself, holding her Oscar in both hands. And there − she felt a sudden catch in her throat − was Arthur, holding up his Oscar triumphantly in one hand. The scene passed swiftly. Now there were closer pan shots.

She saw Jim Edgell, Jack King. Two of the performers who'd appeared in the production number of the Oscar-nominated song from *The Amulet*. Kathleen Havens, who had presented one of the awards.

The scene cut to a wide pan shot across the crowd onstage.

"Here it comes now," Maury said from the back of the screening room.

On-screen one of the figures in the crowd pitched forward and fell to the stage. There was an almost instant zoom-in shot and a close-up of Arthur Strickland lying face-down on the stage, a knife sticking in his back.

"Coming up," Maury called out, "is the stuff I had shot with different cameras, from different angles."

A series of quick cuts appeared: a side view of the crowd onstage as some of the people surged toward where Strickland lay while others scattered backstage and into the wings, an overhead view of the crowd, scenes filmed from the rear of the stage. Halcie, watching closely, was able to pick out a face she recognized here and there, but the cuts were so short and quick that it was similar to trying to register an unfolding scene between the blinks of an eye.

The screen went blank and the lights came on in the screening room.

Staver stood up. "Anybody spot anything? Any hint of who might have done it?"

One of the security men said, "It went awful fast, Lieutenant."

"Yeah." Staver thought so, too. It was a tough break for them that the camera, focused on Strickland when he fell had zoomed in so fast for a close-up of the body that it was impossible to see who was standing directly behind him. Nor had Staver been able to see, from the quick cuts immediately after Strickland fell, who might have been there and tried to move away.

"Let's run it again," he said.

They watched the tape straight through a second time, and when it was finished Staver asked the two security men if either of them had seen the two people who had crashed the ceremonies. Both shook their heads.

Halcie said, "Lieutenant?"

Staver looked at her. "Yes?"

"I didn't see who stabbed him. But I did locate where most of the people who knew him well were standing onstage when he was stabbed. I can point them out to you if we can see the tape again."

Staver nodded. "We might as well get that out of the way, yes."

Maury spoke up, "If it'll help, I can have the projectionist freeze-on-screen whichever scenes you want to study closely."

"Great!" Staver said.

Maury went to the rear of the screening room, spoke to the projectionist, and returned. "Just yell out 'Freeze' when the tape comes to a scene you want to hold on the screen," he said.

They watched the tape of the final number yet another time.

117

"Freeze!" Halcie called out.

The scene remained unmoving on the screen. "There's Arthur — see, in the middle of the stage," she said. "And you can see me to the left, holding my Oscar, three people away from Arthur. Next to the me on one side is Joyce Kimbro. And there's Lewis Worth, president of the Screen Actors Guild, on the other side."

Staver laughed in the darkness as he said, "That's a great relief, Miss Harper. Now I can eliminate you as my chief suspect."

After Maury gave the okay to the projectionist, the tape ran on, stopping at the scenes where Halcie noticed certain individuals she wanted to identify.

Staver was impressed with Halcie's sharp eye. She was even able to spot people in the second row of the crowd from what they were wearing, when otherwise it would have been difficult to identify them because they were partly obscured by figures in the front row.

She pointed out Jack King, standing to the right of Strickland in the first row, and identified the person whose face could not be seen, behind King, as Kathleen Havens because she was wearing a diamond tiara on her head that evening. Courtney, too, was in the second row and blocked from full view by the singer, Young Rose Hightree, who was in the first row, the second person to the left of Strickland. Halcie was able to recognize Courtney because it was possible to see part of her body, most importantly her left hand upon which – as Staver saw when Halcie called attention to it – she wore a ring with a design copied from *The Amulet* ornament she had worn in the film.

Later, in scenes on the tape made after Strickland was stabbed, where Staver could see Kathleen Havens and Courtney Ware clearly, he was able to verify that one wore the tiara and the other the ring.

In still another of the scenes frozen on the screen. Halcie called attention to Jim Edgell in the first row to the right of King, with five people between them. To her surprise she also caught sight of Joan Strickland. She was in the second row behind Joyce Kimbro, who stood two to the right of Strickland.

When Halcie mentioned Joan and where she stood, Maury said, "What was she doing there? She wasn't entitled to appear in the grand finale."

Halcie reminded him that Joan had gone to the stage and stood beside Strickland when he accepted his award. Halcie suggested that Joan had probably simply stayed onstage and mingled with the others for the final number.

Staver had the tape stopped for the first

scenes taken by the other three cameras after Strickland was stabbed. It was still impossible to determine who had been standing directly behind him. Several figures, all photographed from the rear, blocked any clear view of who was standing there; one of those figures seemed to be Jack King, who would, as they knew, be bending over Strickland's body a few seconds later. Another figure seemed to be one of the performers dressed in an Indian costume, who had probably performed in *The Amulet* production number. Still another figure was a man Halcie could not identify.

The tape still hadn't revealed who might have stabbed Strickland.

When the lights came up again in the screening room, Staver asked Maury if he could have a copy of the videotape to study. Maury said he would have a copy run off for him.

Halcie immediately asked, "Ted, may I please have a copy, too? Maybe I can spot something I missed."

Maury agreed he'd have two copies made of the tape. As he started back to the projection booth to arrange for the recordings of the tape so Staver and Halcie could have them when they left, Maury said, "I just thought of something. Those two people who crashed the Awards, you know? I have tapes we made of the

120

crowd out in front of the auditorium before the show began. Any point in looking at what we taped of them?"

"Good idea," Staver said.

They waited until Maury returned from the projection booth.

The lights went out once more, and onto the screen came a series of quick cuts of the scene outside the Dorothy Chandler Pavilion, of the crowd and of the celebrities arriving.

As the scenes appeared, Halcie saw herself arriving with Jack King, and there was a cut to the crowd shouting and cheering, a quick glimpse of Charlton Heston waving to the crowd, another cut to the crowd —

"Hold it! Freeze! Stop the tape!" one of the security guards in the screening room called out.

The tape stopped, leaving on-screen a scene of the crowd cheering.

The security guard hurried from his seat up to the screen. He pointed to a woman clearly visible in the center of the picture.

"It's her!" he said. "She's the one I put out of the place last night."

"You're sure?" Staver asked.

"Positive!" the guard said. "It was right after the end of the show. People were all over the place backstage. I spotted her near an exit door.

121

She didn't look like she belonged there. When I grabbed her, she said she'd just slipped in the exit door. I figured somebody'd gone out and left it open. I put her out. She didn't give me any trouble."

"You're certain it was the same woman?" Staver asked.

"Positive!" the guard said again. "That same dress she had on down to her shoe tops, that flower she wore in her hair. See? Looked like a bag lady to me."

"And you're sure she was just coming in the exit door, not trying to leave?" Staver asked.

"Truthfully," the guard said, "it never occurred to me at the time to think anything but that she'd just walked in. You understand, I didn't know then that anything had happened on the stage."

"So it's possible," Staver said, "that she *could* have been inside earlier and was leaving when you spotted her?"

"It's . . . possible, yeah." The guard nodded his head.

Staver had walked up close to the screen and stood looking at the picture of the woman. He figured that she was in her thirties, maybe forties. Her general appearance was disheveled — the long, loose dress that didn't fit her too well, and the gardenia she wore slightly askew in her hair. He could understand why the guard might have thought she was a bag lady.

"Anybody recognize her?" Staver asked.

No one answered.

One good thing about the picture on the screen was that the woman's face could be seen clearly, Staver thought. They could have photographs made of her face and circulate them. Maybe they'd get an ID on her that way. He made arrangements with Maury to have a print made of the unknown woman, to be sent to him.

Then he said, "Well, I guess that's it." He shook hands with Maury and thanked him for his help.

Maury gave Staver and Halcie copies of the videotapes they'd requested and told Staver he'd send him a print of the unknown woman later in the day.

Staver walked Halcie out to her car. She was using Laura Harrow's limousine and chauffeur. The rain was still coming down hard.

The lieutenant hadn't forgotten that Halcie told him about the threatening notes Strickland had recieved. He wanted to see them without wasting a lot of time arranging for a search warrant. He said, "I wonder, Miss Harper, do you suppose there would be anyone who might know where we could find those threatening messages that were sent to Arthur Strickland?"

"Maggie," Halcie said. "Maggie Geneen, Arthur's assistant. I would think she would know. I can use the car phone and call her."

Staver nodded. "Would you? Please."

Halcie was secretly delighted to continue to be in on the investigation. She got into the waiting limousine quickly, asking the chauffeur, Bradley, to remain parked until she made a phone call.

She found Maggie's number in her address book and called her apartment. When Maggie answered, Halcie explained why she was phoning, and Maggie told her the notes were in the desk in Arthur's study at the house in Bel Air. Maggie said she would like to help in the investigation and suggested that she, Halcie, and the lieutenant meet at Strickland's house.

Staver had remained outside the car, while Halcie made the call. Halcie rolled the car window down and told him what Maggie had said. She gave him the address of Strickland's house.

Staver flipped his cigarette away. "Good! Let's get going. I'll meet you there."

He thought: More to come.

7

Lieutenant Staver looked around the living room of Arthur Strickland's house and wondered at the ego of a man who could have an oil portrait of himself as the centerpiece of the decor.

Staver and Halcie had just come into the house after waiting outside in their cars, the rain coming down hard, until Maggie Geneen arrived. Halcie introduced Staver to Maggie, the three of them standing to close together under Halcie's umbrella that Staver could see only his eyes and Halcie's reflected in the opaque lenses of the large sunglasses Maggie wore.

They were let into the house by Geoffrey, the tall black man who had been with Strickland for years.

"The papers you want are upstairs in Arthur's den," Maggie said to Staver. "Why don't you let Geoffrey show you into the library?"

125

She turned to Halcie. "And why don't you come up with me?"

The two women went up the stairs, and Staver followed Geoffrey across the foyer to a closed door.

"Right in here, sir," Geoffrey said, opening the door.

It was dark in the room for a moment until the houseman switched on the lights. Suddenly, vivid colors leaped out from the walls on all sides of the room from the massive paintings hanging side by side around the oak-paneled library. Beneath the paintings were rows of bookshelves filled with leather-bound volumes.

"Would you care for some coffee, sir?" Geoffrey, standing in the doorway, asked.

"No. Nothing, thanks," Staver said and turned back to look at the paintings.

The houseman withdrew, closing the door behind him.

Staver walked slowly around the room, pausing briefly before each painting, reading the artist's signature. Picasso. Miró. Matisse. Miró. Miró. Picasso. Picasso. Miró. Matisse. Matisse. Matisse. The walls were lined with the works of three artists. One did not have to have any knowledge of art to recognize, from the reality of the colors, that all were originals.

After a while the door to the library opened again, and Halcie and Maggie came in.

"I found the notes," Maggie said. She was holding a manila envelope in her hand.

The three of them gathered around the circular table in the middle of the room, and Maggie opened the envelope and spread the papers out across the tabletop. There were thirteen notes, each stapled to the envelope in which they'd been mailed.

The messages had been printed in crude block letters.

YOU ARE EVIL
GOD WILL PUNISH YOU!

DEATH IS TOO GOOD
FOR YOU!

YOU ARE DOOMED:
GOD WILL PUNISH YOU!

YOU WILL DIE
FOR YOUR SINS!

ARE YOU AFRAID?
BE AFRAID!

THE DATE OF YOUR

DEATH IS NEAR!

ONE DAY SOON
YOU WILL DIE!

I WILL KILL YOU!

THERE'S NO PLACE
FOR YOU TO HIDE!

I'M COMING AFTER
YOU – SOON!

YOUR DAYS ARE
NUMBERED!

I WILL KILL YOU
IN COLD BLOOD!

YOU CAN'T ESCAPE
MY DEADLY WRATH!

The envelopes in which the notes had been mailed were all addressed to Strickland at his office at the studio. The postmarks dated back over a period of eight months.

"How many people knew about these?" Staver asked.

Maggie shrugged. "I don't really know. Arthur told me. I guess he told his lawyer, Henry Bickle. And the police, when Arthur took the notes to them. I do know that he didn't want too many people to learn about them. I didn't even know he'd told Jack King until Halcie told me he had today."

"And he didn't know who might have sent them?"

"He told me he didn't," she said. She explained that Strickland had hired a bodyguard, Paulie Bianco, but had told most people that Paulie was his chauffeur.

"Then you think Mr. Strickland was frightened by the notes?" Staver asked.

"I think he was, at first," she said. "But after time passed and nothing happened, well, I think he just got used to them coming, and thought they were just from some crank. Don't some people in the public eye, as Arthur was, sometimes get such threats?"

"Sometimes." He nodded. "I'd like to take the notes with me."

"I guess that's all right," Maggie said slowly. "After all, he did take them to the police once himself."

She put the notes back into the manila envelope and handed the envelope to him.

He looked at Halcie. "I think I'd like to talk

129

to Jack King, see if Strickland happened to tell him anything more about these notes."

Halcie saw her opportunity to continue to be involved in the investigation. "It just so happens," she said, "that Jack and I are meeting for lunch at twelve-thirty at the Bel Air Hotel. Why don't you join us?"

Staver glanced at his watch. "I guess I could." He nodded. "There are a couple of things I have to do first, but I can meet you there."

He thanked Maggie for her help, and as the three of them started to leave the library, the door opened, and Joan Strickland and Henry Bickle stood there.

"Hell-o-o," Joan said sweetly. "Geoffrey told us you were in here." She came in through the door, followed by the lawyer.

Halcie again made the introductions to the lieutenant, and explained to Joan why she, Staver, and Maggie were there.

Joan continued to smile sweetly, turning her head to glance at Bickle, who was frowning.

"Lieutenant — Staver, is it?" Bickle said. "Isn't your visit a bit unorthodox?"

"I wouldn't say that," Staver said easily. "Informal, maybe. I just learned about the threatening notes Mr. Strickland had been receiving. I believe you know about them. I wanted to see them. I didn't see any harm in that, especially since I knew Mr. Strickland himself had once taken them to the police."

"And do you have a search warrant?" the lawyer asked. "You realize, don't you, that this is now Mrs. Strickland's house?"

"No, I didn't realize that." Staver turned slightly and looked at Joan Strickland. "That's very interesting."

Joan put a hand on Bickle's sleeve. "It's all right, Henry."

"No." The lawyer shook his head. "It's not all right. There are proper ways of doing things — "

"Fine," Staver said, holding out the manilla envelope. "Take them, and I'll get a search warrant and you can give them back to me." He ignored the lawyer and looked at Joan. "Is that what you want?"

Joan shook her head. "It's all right, Lieutenant. I want you to keep them."

"Thank you." Staver looked at the lawyer. "Mr. Bickle?"

Bickle waved a hand in the air. "If that's what Mrs. Strickland wants . . ."

Staver started to leave, and so did Halcie and Maggie. Joan said to the two women, "Please stay for a bit, have some coffee or a drink." And, addressing Bickle, she added, "You'll excuse us, won't you, Henry? I'll speak to you later in the day."

Joan left the room to walk Staver and Bickle to the door.

Halcie looked at Maggie, now that they were alone, and said softly, "I'm so sorry, my dear. I'm afraid, by asking for your help for the lieutenant, I've placed you in an awkward situation."

Maggie removed her sunglasses for the first time that day. Her eyes looked like two red, raw wounds in the center of her face, bloodshot and swollen from crying. "I don't care!" she said fiercely. "I care only that whoever killed Arthur gets caught. That's all that matters!"

Halcie understood Maggie's great anger at the death of the man she loved. Halcie remembered her own terrible sense of loss, of grief — yes, even of anger, when David died, and his was a peaceful death.

They could hear Joan returning through the hall to the library.

Maggie covered her eyes again with the dark sunglasses.

"I felt so sorry for Maggie," Halcie said to Jack King at lunch at the Bel Air Hotel while they waited for Lieutenant Staver to arrive.

"Can you imagine? She had to sit there and listen while Joan went on and on about how life works in such mysterious ways, as she put it.

She and Arthur would have been divorced by now *if* there hadn't been financial problems on finishing *The Amulet* and she hadn't put up the money he needed. A condition of which was that he not change the will he made while they were married and living together. That will left her the house *and* Arthur G. Strickland Productions. Keeping the will intact was her protection until he repaid the loan. And now, after his senseless murder, it's all hers, which shows, as she kept repeating, how life works in such mysterious ways."

King said, "Yeah, I'll bet Maggie would agree with that now, too."

"The really terrible part for Maggie," Halcie went on, "is that she not only had to sit there and listen to all she lost because the divorce hadn't gone through and Arthur hadn't married her, but she couldn't reveal her deep grief at Arthur's death. Even though both Joan and Maggie knew the truth, and knew that the other knew it, they put on a show of pretending it wasn't so."

"So," King said, "even if Joan didn't stick the knife in Arthur, she certainly stuck it in Maggie, from what you say."

Halcie nodded. "And when Joan told us that she was going to take over Arthur's company and produce the film Jim Edgell's writing, she said ever so nicely that she wanted Maggie to stay on in, as Joan put it, 'some capacity or other.' "

"Gofer, probably," King murmured.

Halcie laughed. "Oh," she said. "Joan also informed us that according to Arthur's will, it was his wish that he be cremated and that there be no services for him."

"That would be typical of Arthur." King winked. "He wouldn't want to be a party to any affair where he couldn't have the last word."

Halcie laughed again.

King laughed, too, and said, "Actually, I remember once Arthur and I had a passing discussion about funerals. Something about some funeral Arthur had to attend and didn't want to. I told him my feelings: that I didn't go to weddings anymore and I didn't go to funerals because I didn't approve of people marrying and I certainly didn't approve of people dying. Maybe he remembered my words and wrote his instructions accordingly, for me."

Halcie shook her head with a laugh. "Jack, you're incorrigible."

"Yes." He nodded. "I suppose you could say that." More seriously, he added, "Halcie, if we do go on with the film of *Misplaced Affection*, you'll sign on, won't you? The role's perfect for you, you know."

"The fact is," Halcie said, "I haven't had time to think about it. Until Joan told us her plans, I'd just assumed that with Arthur dead, the movie wouldn't be made. I haven't even looked at the script yet."

"You'll like it," King said firmly. "If you do the film, it'll give you a chance to stick around until Arthur's murder is solved, in case the thought hasn't occured to you."

Halcie gave him a sideways glance. "You're pretty sharp, aren't you, Mr. Director?"

He grinned.

Halcie, looking past him, said, "Speaking of solving Arthur's murder, here comes Lieutenant Staver."

Halcie had already told King about the lieutenant. King hadn't minded that she had told Staver her information about the threatening notes Strickland had received had come from him. King said, "The truth is I would have told the police myself if I'd remembered. I just never thought about them."

Staver approached the table, and King stood up as Halcie said, "Lieutenant Staver, Jack King."

King liked Staver's looks. The lieutenant was in his late thirties, dark-haired, medium height. He had a strong, serious face that could still produce a friendly smile, and an easy manner.

King immediately felt comfortable with him and decided, knowing he was a detective, that his looks were right for the role.

"Nice to meet you, Mr. King," Staver said. "I hope I'm not intruding."

"Not at all." King motioned to a chair. "Miss Harper told me about you, about the investigation. Anything I can do to help, just ask."

"Thanks. I appreciate your offer."

The waiter had followed Staver to the table and stayed while they ordered lunch.

Staver took out a handkerchief and wiped a few wet spots off the side of his face, saying, "Some rain we're having."

King laughed suddenly, shaking his head. "I just remembered a conversation with Arthur a couple of nights ago. He was telling Miss Harper she ought to move out here, get some sun."

"I remember," Halcie said, smiling.

Staver put his handkerchief away. "Tell me what Mr. Strickland had to say about the threatening notes he was getting."

"We only discussed them once," King said. "It was right after he hired Paulie Bianco as his bodyguard, disguised as chauffeur. Arthur explained hiring Paulie by telling me about the notes. It wasn't a long conversation. We were alone in his office at the studio after a meeting we'd had about the new movie we were going to make, *Misplaced Affection.* He'd received one of the notes earlier that day, and I guess the whole business was on his mind."

Staver nodded. "Did he show you the note, or the notes?"

"He did. One of the notes, the one he'd received that day. It said something like, 'You are going to die.' Something like that. All printed in big letters. I asked him if it was a joke. He said no, because he'd gotten other such messages."

"And that was the only time he mentioned the notes to you?"

"The only time, yes."

"It may be," Staver said, "that the threats had nothing to do with his murder. I sent the notes to the crime lab to be checked out. But chances are they won't tell us anything about who sent them."

"You still have the videotapes, though," Halcie said.

"Oh, we'll be looking at them closely." Staver leaned back in his chair, relaxed as he glanced around the room. "I was born and raised in L.A.," he said. "I've always heard about the famous Bel Air Hotel and must have driven past it, what, a thousand, two thousand times in my life. Today's the first time I've been inside."

Still glancing around the room, he then said, "A thing that puzzles me about this case — I hear Strickland and his wife were planning to divorce and that Maggie Geneen, his assistant, was his sweet . . . whatever. And *they* planned to marry."

Staver looked back at King, and at Halcie.

Halcie was surprised; obviously Staver hadn't known these facts earlier when they were at Strickland's house, with Joan and Maggie. She was sure of that. If he had known, she'd bet he would have quizzed the two women, one way or another. He had talked to someone else after he'd left her at Strickland's house.

Staver noted that Halcie realized he knew more about the affairs of Arthur Strickland now than he had earlier in the day. That fact was due to Detective Murch. The previous night, at the Awards ceremonies, Murch had spoken briefly with newspaper columnist Didi Jones and discovered she knew most of the inside gossip about Strickland. She had agreed to meet and talk with him the next morning. When Staver left Halcie at Strickland's house, he sat in on the conversation between Murch and Jones at her house in Century City.

The columnist told them everything she'd heard about Strickland, providing them with a number of possible leads. In exchange, she said she hoped they would give her the news first when they made an arrest in the case. Staver made her no promises but assured her they would remember the help she had given them.

Staver waited until they finished the meeting and were outside the house to give Murch the videotape to take back to the precinct and the threatening notes to take to the crime lab.

Now, in the Bel Air Hotel, Staver continued his comments about Joan Strickland and Maggie Geneen. "As I understand it, Joan knew about her husband's plans to marry Maggie. Yet when we were all together, earlier today, who would have guessed it, observing them together? They both sure put on a great act, I'd say."

King raised an eyebrow. "As you probably know better than I, Lieutenant, appearances can be deceiving."

Staver nodded. "It's only that it doesn't make a case like this any easier to crack."

King said softly, "I suspect you're going to find, in the course of your investigation, that Arthur was a complex person who led a complicated life. And the same is true of most of the people who were around him."

"You mean because he was a movie producer?"

"Because he was a *successful* movie producer,"

King said. "He made money, he had power; inevitably, now and then, he made enemies."

"Certainly one particular enemy," Staver said. He looked at Halcie. "Yet you liked him, Miss Harper, I think."

"Yes. I did." Halcie nodded. "There was another quality about Arthur: he also had a great deal of charm. I suppose I was lucky that mostly I saw only that side of him."

Staver turned his attention toward King. "And you, Mr. King? You worked with him; how did you feel about him?"

King laughed easily. "Perhaps not as charming as Miss Harper found him to be. We had our battles. But we got along. You see, Arthur and I both wanted to make motion pictures, and together we made them. That went a long way toward settling any differences we might have had from time to time."

"Arthur was serious about making movies," Halcie said. "Absolutely."

Staver looked puzzled. "Is that so unusual in your business?"

Half kidding, King said, "I will tell you that sometimes there's such irrational behavior in making films that I have secretly speculated if the damn drug problem hadn't come along to blame in part, somebody would have to invent another explanation."

Staver and Halcie laughed.

"Of course," King added, "for all I know, the same irrational behavior may exist in other businesses . . . in Wall Street."

King grinned, paused for a moment, and said, "Have we satisfied you, Lieutenant? That neither Miss Harper nor I had reason to want Arthur dead? That's really what this meeting is all about, isn't it?"

The waiter brought their lunch. Staver didn't answer until they'd been served.

"In a murder investigation," he said, "and this is just the beginning of the investigation, the way it is, is you keep asking questions until finally you discover where the truth lies."

8

Staver took the lid off his cup of coffee and picked up the morning newspaper Detective Tomasini had left on his desk. The paper was opened to the Didi Jones gossip column. Staver sipped his coffee and read:

ALL OF HOLLYWOOD IS BUZZING ABOUT: the new movie, "Misplaced Affection," which begins filming this morning by Arthur G. Strickland Productions, barely one week after Arthur Strickland was fatally stabbed at the Oscar Awards. ("While Arthur's ashes are still warm," said one Hollywood wit of Strickland, who was cremated.) Joan Strickland, Arthur's widow, who inherited the production company, is the producer of the new film, which stars Courtney Ware and Halcie Harper. Jack King is directing, and the script was written by James Edgell. All four won Oscars a week ago for the last film they did together, "The Amulet." Meanwhile, L.A. police have made no arrests in the mysterious murder, although the rumor is that they are swamped by tips from individuals all over the world who taped their own videocassettes of the Oscar show and who believe they have spotted the murderer. Now the new parlor game the whole world is playing is Who Killed Arthur G. Strickland?

Staver shook his head. If there was one thing the investigation didn't need now, it was an announcement in the newspapers that the public was trying to figure out Strickland's murderer by watching videotapes of the Academy Awards. The switchboard at the precinct was already so jammed with calls from people who thought they'd solved the case that extra operators had been hired. The column by Didi Jones would only encourage even more people to report their theories. Staver knew well that almost everyone felt challenged to play detective; what else, he had often thought, could account for the great popularity of fictional murder mysteries!

All the media, TV, radio, newspapers, recognized the murder was a sensational story. Every

TV news show kept running film clips of the stabbing, the papers were full of stories and photographs of the scene at the Oscars, and the case was the first item on the radio news reports. The Mayor was pressing for a speedy solution to the murder.

He lit a cigarette and thought that while it was true that they hadn't made an arrest in the case yet, they had accumulated a mass of information about Strickland's death, his life, and even about the lives of many of the people around him. Some of the information had possible value, some was worthless.

The coroner's report revealed that the knife blade had plunged through the left side of Strickland's back, near the top of the rib cage, and penetrated deep into the aorta. The coroner's opinion was that death had been instantaneous.

The police lab had no significant findings to report on the murder weapon, the knife itself. It was not new and had no markings on it. The steel blade was seven and a quarter inches in length and had a two-inch curve on top just before it came to a point. It had been recently sharpened and the tip filed. The bone handle was three inches long. There were no fingerprints on the handle or blade. Staver had no real hope that the knife would provide them with any possible clue to the identity of the killer.

About the only information the crime lab had been able to establish about the anonymous death threats sent to Strickland was that all of them, along with the envelopes, had been written by the same person. They were unable to recover any fingerprints from the paper on which the notes had been written or from the envelopes.

Photographs had been made of the unknown woman on the videotape who was thought to have been ejected by the security guards at the auditorium, and copies were being circulated throughout the LAPD with a request that the woman be detained if sighted.

There was no information about the other person, the unknown man, who had also been evicted from the ceremonies by a security guard.

During the past five days, detectives on Staver's Homicide Task Force had tracked down and questioned those people who had taken part in the Oscar show but had left by the time the police arrived. No new facts had emerged from interrogations of those people.

Also during the past five days, Staver and his team had been sorting through the boxes of papers and documents they had seized and removed from Strickland's den in Bel Air and office at the New Centurion Studios. On the afternoon of the same day that Staver visited Strickland's house with Halcie and was given the threatening notes, he had obtained a search warrant, and he and several other detectives had recovered the dead man's files before anyone could remove or destroy the records.

Since then the detectives had spent hours looking through the files of letters, contracts, financial statements, canceled checks, duplicate income tax returns, memos, and notes. It was not an easy task, both because Strickland had kept records of almost every social and business transaction in which he had been involved and because they were searching at random for any information they could piece together that might give them a lead.

In addition to all the documents Strickland had had in his house and in his office, Staver suspected that somewhere there existed a safe or a safe deposit box belonging to him.

One thing the lieutenant had learned for sure was that Jack King hadn't been overstating the truth when he said Strickland would probably be found to be a complex man who led a complicated life.

Then there was the particular irony about the murder: the videotape with the very act permanently recorded at the instant it happened. Yet, although Staver and the men in his squad had viewed the tape over and over again, they still had found no clue to the identity of the killer.

Staver was not, however, discouraged. He knew the real investigative work was still ahead. In the coming days he and the rest of the homicide team would be interrogating everyone they could uncover who had ever known Strickland. Somewhere among them would be the killer.

He finished his coffee, reached for one of the files containing a bulk of letters they'd found in Strickland's den, and the phone rang. He put out his cigarette and answered the phone on the second ring.

"Lieutenant Staver, Homicide Task Force."

"Lieutenant, this is Halcie Harper. I hope I'm not bothering you."

"Good morning, Miss Harper. Didn't I read in the paper that you were starting a new movie this morning?"

"I am. I'm phoning you from the studio while they're setting up the first shot. I think I have another piece of information for you about Arthur's murder."

"Yes, go on."

"It's about the videotape. Perhaps you already know what I'm talking about."

"No, I'm afraid I don't. What about it?"

"Oh, good! Then I *am* being helpful. I

thought you might have caught it on the tape when you watched it again."

"What was it that I should have caught, Miss Harper?"

She lowered her voice conspiratorially: "That at the time Arthur was stabbed there was one more individual on stage made up as an Indian than there was when *The Amulet* number was performed earlier — one more individual disguised as an Indian than there should have been, according to Ted Maury's list of people who were part of the show."

"You're *sure* about this?"

"Oh, yes! You'll see it for yourself when you look at the tape again. You can count the people who took part in the number; there are twenty-two singers and dancers. Later, on the tape made directly after Arthur was stabbed, you can clearly see that there are twenty-three people in *Amulet* costumes and makeup."

"And you're certain that twenty-two is the number on Ted Maury's list?"

"I double-checked with him before I called you."

"Miss Harper?"

"Yes?"

"How in the world did you ever think to count up the number of those particular people at the different times they were onstage?"

Her voice was delighted when she answered: "Laura Harrow, my friend – I'm staying with her, you know – we made another tape for her. And she's been watching it over and over, and I've been watching my tape over and over. And we decided at one point that we'd do a count of *all* the people in costume in *all* the production numbers. We decided if there was one more person in costume onstage later when Arthur was stabbed, the costume would be a disguise. It turned out that there *was* one extra person in an Indian costume than there had been in *The Amulet* production number."

"I'm – really grateful for your help, Miss Harper," Staver said. "Thank you."

"You're welcome, Lieutenant."

"Oh, and Miss Harper, don't tell anyone else about this, will you?"

"No, I won't. You don't have to worry about that. God bless."

"Good-bye."

Staver hung up and called into his office Murch, Tomasini, and Cooney, who were the only members of the task force in the outside squad room at the time. He told them about the call from Halcie Harper.

They played the tape again on the VCR they'd rented. They saw that she was right.

"This will be a take," Jack King said.

"Quiet! Quiet on the set," the assistant director, Mark Whelan, yelled. "This is a take."

"Roll 'em."

King prowled back and forth in the darkness at the edge of the lighted studio set, watching again the opening scene of *Misplaced Affection* as the cameras filmed. This was the eleventh take they'd done of the same scene.

The set was of the passenger lounge at JFK Airport in New York, where the characters portrayed by Halcie and Courtney meet for the first time when the plane each has planned to take to Los Angeles is grounded by bad weather. Also in the scene was the young actress, Zoe Rushell, who in the film was going to L.A. to be married.

Strickland had had the set constructed in preparation for the movie before he was killed.

As the action began, Halcie was sitting in the lounge reading a book when Courtney entered. Halcie glanced up and smiled, Courtney smiled back.

"It's still a real blizzard out there," Courtney said, and looked off. "I noticed you earlier at the reservation window; I think we're both booked on the same flight — if it ever takes off."

"Yes, we are on the same plane," Halcie said. "I noticed you, too, dear. Why don't you sit down. You might as well relax."

As Courtney moved to sit, Zoe came hurrying into the lounge and began talking nonstop, pacing back and forth all the while.

"Can you believe it! Of all the dumb things to happen! A blizzard! I mean, I've been planning for this day for months and here I am stuck in an airport! And *he's* out there in sunny Hollywood waiting to marry me —"

"Cut!" King called out from the darkness. "Zoe, the line is 'sunny California.' "

Zoe stamped her foot hard and said, "Oh, damn! Mr. King, I'm sorry. I knew I had blown the line the minute I said it."

"It's all right, it's all right," King said soothingly as he walked onto the set.

Zoe, in near tears, looked at Halcie and Courtney, and said, "I'm really sorry, really."

Both women smiled back encouragingly.

"Don't worry, dear," Halcie said.

"It happens to all of us," Courtney said.

King crossed to Zoe and put a hand on her shoulder. "You're doing fine. I think the real problem is that you have more lines than you can keep track of in this scene."

She shook her head miserably. "But I *know* my lines. Why do they keep coming out of my mouth wrong?"

King said, "What we're going to do is fix it.

151

And the way we're going to do it is put all your lines in this scene on cue cards. Okay?"

She nodded her head.

"Good!" King turned his head and called out loudly. "Lunch break, everybody! One hour and back on the set!"

He walked over to Halcie as the others on the set began to leave and some of the lights went down.

Halcie stood up. King put his arm around her shoulders. "How you doing?"

"You mustn't fret about me, Jack," Halcie said. "You and I have been through all this before."

"Yeah." He thought for a moment. "Do me a favor, Halcie?"

"Certainly."

"Would you and Courtney take Zoe to lunch at the commissary? The three of you have lunch together. You know, to let her get to know both of you a little better. I think she's a bit overawed at working with the two of you."

"Of course," Halcie said. "You think that's the trouble?"

"I think," King said carefully, "things are a trifle out of sync on the set today. Not exactly unexpected, considering Arthur's death, the fact that we're shooting with an unfinished script" — he looked over toward where Joan

Strickland, who had been observing the filming from behind the cameras, now stood talking to Zoe — "not to mention that we're working under an inexperienced producer."

King watched Joan for a moment and added, "You know that old truth about making movies: 'Those who can act, do; those who can't, direct; and those who can do neither, produce,' " which brought a laugh from Halcie.

Zoe was excited. "Excuse me, Miss Harper, do you mean *the* Clark Gable?"

"Oh, yes," Halcie said, amused. "*The* Clark Gable. This was a long time ago, you understand, when we made the movie together."

Halcie glanced around the studio commissary, which was crowded, glanced at Zoe and Courtney, and continued the story she was telling.

She and Clark Gable were starring in a movie set in Austria in the 1800's. The big scene was a festival in the town square — dozens of extras, she and Gable all in fancy costumes, flowers everywhere, a small band playing.

"The setting was on the studio back lot, of course," Halcie said, "and it was a difficult scene to shoot because of all the extras."

They kept shooting the scene over and over again all through the day to get it right, and

153

even into the night. In between takes, she would rest in her chair behind the camera. The night kept getting colder and colder.

Halcie shook her head, remembering. "It was an ordeal. One of the wardrobe people noticed how cold I was and brought my fur coat to put around me while I rested between the takes."

Finally, close to midnight, when it seemed that all the problems had been wroked out, they did yet another take, and were relieved when the director at last said the scene had worked beautifully and they could wrap it up for the night.

"I started to leave the set," Halcie said, "when I suddenly realized — with horror, I assure you — that all during that last take I had forgotten to slip out of my fur coat. What they had filmed was me there in this bulky fur coat while every woman around me in the scene had on a gauzy summery gown."

Courtney put a hand over her face. "What did you *do?*"

Halcie laughed. "What *could* I do? I had to tell the director. He couldn't believe it because he hadn't noticed. The cameramen hadn't, either. In fact, not one person on the set had noticed. But when I convinced them — and later, the next day, they knew I was right when they saw the rushes — why, we shot the scene over again, finishing in the early-morning hours. My goodness, what a night that was!"

All three women laughed. Halcie put her hand over Zoe's hand. "So, you see, my dear, this morning was no real problem."

After Halcie, Courtney, and Zoe left the set, King spent some time arranging with the script girl to have Zoe's dialogue put on cue cards. When he finished, he found himself confronted by Joan Strickland. She was frowning. "Not a very fruitful morning, would you say, Jack?"

He took a cigar from his pocket and began unwrapping it. "We'll make it up, Joan."

"If you think Zoe has too many lines in the scene, as I heard you say, have you thought of asking Jim Edgell to cut some of them?"

"No. No, I haven't. All those lines, coming nonstop, are setting up her character in the film. I told you we'd work it out, Joan. It's early yet."

"Maybe it's early yet," Joan said, "but it's later than it was this morning when we started. And we haven't accomplished anything."

King shrugged; he really didn't have an additional answer. She was going to have to learn, from experience, that what he said was true.

He had walked her to the studio exit as they

talked. He knew she detested the odor of cigars and thought that was probably why Arthur used to smoke them.

"We're going to have a terrific film here, Joan," he told her and lit his cigar.

"I hope so," she said and hurried away.

He walked out of the studio, smoking his cigar, and went toward the studio back lot.

The day was hot and humid, a low-lying smog hanging over the city, after the drenching rains they'd had only a week earlier. King took off his jacket and slung it over his shoulder.

There was bustling activity on the studio lot all around him. Eight television shows were filming at the studio and two feature films in addition to *Misplaced Affection.*

King enjoyed getting away alone and strolling through the studio back lot during breaks in the shooting. Despite all the upheavals and changes in the movie business over the years, there were several famous film sets still standing on the studio lot from an earlier era.

He walked slowly past a set of gothic columns and spires and a marble staircase that led upward to nowhere. These basic elements of the set had been constructed for a film that years ago was begun but never finished. The columns, spires, and staircase had remained, however, and, with the addition of various backdrops, had appeared in a dozen or more other movies through the years. It proved Hollywood had the know-how to recycle its sets along with its movie plots.

He went on until he reached another set, a towering fake clay hill that rose high into the air at the very back of the studio lot. The hill had been used in several Western films, a couple of war films, and a film supposedly set in the Deep South.

He slowly climbed the hill until he reached a spot near the top where years earlier he had discovered there was a fake boulder he could sit on. From there he could look down on the roofs of the studio buildings and the tops of the other sets. Beyond the walls of the studio he could see for a distance the sprawl of the surrounding hills and streets and buildings of Los Angeles, the umbrella-inside-out shape of the crowns of the palm trees lining the boulevards and, up above, a silver jetliner climbing toward the sky, adding its streams of vapor to the smog into which it disappeared.

He sat, smoking his cigar, and thought about the movie they had just begun to film. There were going to be more than the usual problems, more than the usual tension on the set because of Joan's presence as producer, because of Arthur's unsolved murder and the climate of suspicion it created among all of them.

It was really a mistake, he thought, to have started work on the new film so quickly. Jim Edgell still hadn't completed revisions on the screenplay. But Joan had been insistent. And she had them all under contract. She had made it clear that each of them would do the movie or she would go ahead and do it without them.

King believed he understood part of her reasoning; because of Arthur's murder, they were all very much in the public eye, and she wanted to capitalize on that fact. The public would flock to see the new film. It was a form of exploiting the murder, he supposed, but, hell, the same kind of thing was done so often every day, everywhere, that it had become the norm in the entertainment marketplace. Convicted murderers, mobsters, embezzlers of widows and orphans, corrupt politicians – all had their books published, TV miniseries or movies made, became freak celebrities of the media. It was all due to the public's curiosity, which, he had to believe, no longer killed the cat so much as it sweetened the kitty.

He thought about the column by Didi Jones he'd read in the morning newspaper. And he wondered: Who *had* killed Arthur G. Strickland?

9

Paulie Bianco said, "Look, Lieutenant, I don't know anything, not any - thing, more about who might have killed Mr. Strickland than I already told your detective when he questioned me at the Oscars."

"Sure," Staver said, nodding in agreement. "I believe you believe that. On the other hand, I thought we should talk. Maybe you'd remember something else, before you took off and we didn't know where to find you."

Paulie edged forward in the chair on the opposite side of the desk from Staver. "See, that's another thing. You think I was packing up and checking out because of something to do with his murder. But like I told the detective you sent to my place to bring me in, Mrs. Strickland, the widow, fired me. Said she didn't need a chauffeur or a bodyguard. I figured it was time to go back to Chicago." He spread his hands. "That's all there was to it."

Staver nodded again and put his feet up against a corner of the desk, rocking back in his chair.

They'd found out that Paulie had been fired when Murch went to the Strickland house to talk to the butler, Geoffrey. He had given them Paulie's address and, as soon as Staver heard Paulie was no longer working there, he'd instructed Murch to pick him up and bring him in for questioning.

Staver looked Paulie in the eye and said, "We know you have a police record."

Paulie sat up straighter in the chair. "That's ancient history. I'm square. I did my time. Besides, the whole thing was a misunderstanding. The sentence was later commuted."

"That doesn't change the fact that a jury believed you were guilty of aggravated assault and attempted murder."

"You want to hear the true facts?" Paulie took a deep breath. "Okay, then. Eight, nine, years ago, it was. I took a job with this woman over in Pasadena. She was very rich. My job was the same setup I just had with Mr. Strickland — chauffeur-bodyguard, mostly the latter. She and her husband were separated, she claimed he was violent, slapped her around a lot. She wanted a divorce, he didn't. She claimed he still kept threatening her, phone calls and letters. She got a court order that he was to leave her alone. But he didn't. So she hired me to protect her. All this is a part of the transcript of my trial, if you want to look it up."

Staver nodded. "Okay, go on."

"About a month after I started working for her, I bring her home late one night after a concert. I let her out of the car in the driveway and get back into the car to park it in the garage. I lived in a small apartment over the garage, you know?"

Staver nodded again, letting him talk.

Paulie continued. "She's out of the car and she gets about halfway to the door of the house and suddenly I hear her scream. I see this guy, bigger than a Rams linebacker, has come rushing out of the shadows and jumped her. I figured it was her husband, which later I found out it was. I run to help her. By that time he's punched her head back and forth like a punching bag. He's got her down on the ground, one hand over her mouth to cut off her screams, the other around her throat, choking her."

Paulie was quiet for a moment, his face mournful at the memory.

"I'm there then, trying to drag him off of her," he went on. "So he drops her and turns on me. I mean, this guy's a wild man! He's throwing everything he's got at me. I think he's going to beat me to death. I fight back. I mean, I was fighting for my life. I guess that's all that saved me. He hits me and hits me and hits me, and I hit him and hit him and hit him. I go down, he goes down, we both keep getting up, me because I figure if I stay down, it's the end for me. We're both taking a terrible beating. Finally, he goes down and is slow getting up, and I manage to get on top of him and pin his arms down with both my legs. Still, he won't give up. I have to keep punching and punching until I knock him unconscious. And then the cops came."

"If that's what happened, how come the jury found you guilty?" Staver asked.

Paulie raised a hand. "Wait. You haven't heard even the half of it. Just before the cops came, having been called by the neighbors, I get one good look at the wife as she's staggering on into the house. She's all beat up. One side of her face is all ballooned out and she can hardly move. Anyhow, the cops are there and they take the husband and me to the hospital, both of us under guard, until they can find out what happened."

Staver lit a cigarette, waiting for Paulie to go on.

"At the hospital," Paulie said, "they patch me up and give me something to knock me out. When I wake up, I find I'm charged with

162

aggravated assault and attempted murder. And they transfer me from the hospital to jail. I can't believe what's going on! They say the guy claimed he'd gone to the house to speak to his wife and that I had come at him like a maniac and, with no provocation — I'll always remember that phrase, 'with no provocation' — beat him half to death."

"You mean the police didn't talk to the wife?" Staver asked. "And how about at the trial?"

"I told you before," Paulie said, grinning. "You still haven't heard the half of it. That night it happened the police couldn't get to the wife because before they could, she'd blocked them from her with her lawyer and her doctor. Both said that night she was 'too emotionally distraught' to talk to the police directly. The next day, after her lawyer heard what the husband claimed had happened, the lawyer told the police the wife backed up her husband's story."

He stopped talking, and Staver asked, "You're not going to tell me again that I haven't heard the half of it, are you? What about at the trial? What did the wife say then?"

"The same thing," Paulie said. "She was a witness for the prosecution. You understand, by then she was all healed from the beating he'd given her that night. Nobody ever saw at the trial the way she looked that night. The husband testified, too, of course, claiming the same thing he'd told the police when they first questioned him. Between the stories of the two of them, naturally the jury found me guilty as charged."

Staver looked hard at him. "So actually, it was just your word against theirs, then and now. Which still leaves the question I have to ask you: Why would the wife back up her husband's story if everything you've told me is true?"

"Man, you know how many times I asked myself that same question after I was in jail? And, besides all that, while I was doing time, I heard from my lawyer, who visited me a couple of times, that they — the husband and wife — went back together again."

Paulie half grinned again. "It was about six months before I got the whole answer. I read it first in the papers in jail. One day, after they'd been back together for about six months, she shot him dead. She claimed he'd tried to beat her, threatened to kill her, and she shot him in self-defense."

He looked straight at Staver. "You get it now, don't you? As she'd expected, they had to bring her to trial. This time she produced photographs of herself showing the damage he'd inflicted upon her the night I had to beat him up. I was brought from jail to testify for her. I told the same story I told at my own trial. The jury freed her. Shortly thereafter, the powers that be commuted my sentence without comment."

Staver asked, "Wasn't any question raised at her trial about why she testified against you at your trial?"

Paulie gave a wave of his hand. "She was asked, like in passing. She said something about she guessed she was confused, didn't really understand what had happened, that she had more or less believed what her husband had said about that night and hoped maybe they could still make a go of their marriage. Nobody made a big deal about what she said, or didn't say, at my trial. Mostly, I guess, because nobody really cared that she shot and killed the miserable bastard, and nobody really wanted her to go to jail. Including me. She'd figured out that he was going to get her sooner or later, so she had to get him first. I think she figured out exactly how she was going to do it, and get away with it, the very night he beat me up and I beat him up."

"That's a hell of an interesting story," Staver said, meaning it.

Paulie relaxed in the chair. "Yeah. Mr. Strickland liked it, too, when I told it to him. He said the plot might be good enough to write a story about it. Changing the facts. You know, like

165

somebody wants to kill somebody only they don't plan out the whole thing. And then, one day, they just do it — bam! You see what I mean?"

"Sure." Staver rubbed his chin. "You mean, it's premeditated murder, only it's committed on the spur of the moment."

"Like that, yeah."

"I'm sure it's happened, at times," Staver said. Then he added, "You think that's what happened to Arthur Strickland? Somebody had a motive for killing him but didn't plan how to do it until an opportunity presented itself at the Oscars?"

"I wouldn't know about that," Paulie said carefully.

Staver dropped his feet from the corner of the desk and swung upright in his chair. "I heard when you first went to work for Strickland, he promised to give you a role in his new movie, *Misplaced Affection*. I heard that just recently he told you you weren't going to have a role in the film after all. And you were pretty sore about it."

"Hey! Hey! Hey!" Paulie said anxiously. "I wasn't *that* sore. To kill him. I know where you got that story — from his new girlfriend. I heard him tell her once when I was driving them. Well, she's dead wrong."

Actually, Murch had been given the informa-

166

tion by Geoffrey, but Staver didn't correct him. He'd learned a long time ago that in an interrogation you let the subject of the grilling do the talking, with a minimum of prompting. He supposed when Paulie had said new girlfriend, he meant Maggie Geneen. But all Staver asked was, "Who?"

"His new girlfriend, that Zoe Rushell," Paulie said, wanting to show how shrewd he was. "You can't fool me. I know she was the one who told you."

Well, Staver thought, there it was: a new fact added, like a word in an incomplete crossword puzzle, that might or might not lead to the correct solution.

He dismissed Paulie, telling him curtly he had a choice of staying in town or of being booked and held as a material witness. Paulie said he wasn't exactly surprised to hear this news and that he'd already decided while they were talking that he might as well stay around L.A. for a while and collect his unemployment insurance.

Staver was glad to get rid of him. He didn't know whether he would have, or could have, held him, but he figured it wouldn't hurt to throw a scare into him. What he really wanted to do, now that he had learned Zoe Rushell had been Strickland's new girlfriend, was to set up some kind of arrangement where he could be present when the whole group that had been close to Strickland was together. He knew exactly who could help him accomplish such an arrangement: Halcie Harper.

So far this day the filming on *Misplaced Affection* had gone smoothly, much to Jack King's relief. For several days they had been shooting on location out on the Sunset Strip where they had taken over the popular restaurant Tulli's, redecorated the facade, and given it a new name, Ariel's for the movie, complete with a sign in front.

The company had a police permit for the outdoor filming, and there were cops present to keep back the crowd when they'd filmed the exterior scenes earlier. Reporters and TV news teams, who were still running stories on the murder, had also collected at the scene to gather material for their readers and viewers, which added to the problems of the police.

They'd already shot most of the sequence inside the restaurant.

In the sequence, which was one of King's favorites in the script, the character of the kooky young girl, played by Zoe, had decided to act as matchmaker for the characters portrayed by Courtney and Halcie. She had tricked them into a dinner where she and her boy-friend had brought along two men, a young man for Courtney, an older gentlemen for Halcie.

Both Courtney and Halcie were embarrassed that Zoe had brought dates for them, since both really wanted to be alone now that they had lost their husbands, Courtney's who had died, Halcie's who had left her.

All six of the diners were ill at ease and tried unsuccessfully to relieve the awkwardness, while Zoe, as usual, cheerily talked nonstop throughout the scene as if they were all old friends.

King thought there was humor in the dialogue Edgell had scripted for Zoe, a free-association flow of observations, reminiscences, and outrageous opinions.

"What I like about California, as opposed to New York," Edgell had had Zoe say, "is you can't walk everywhere you're going. In New York people are always walking, so nobody's ever at home. Even when they're home, everybody's always popping out suddenly to walk somewhere. It's so easy to just walk somewhere, people don't think about are they going to do something, they just get up and walk and do it. You call them on the phone and all you get is their answering machine. Out here, when you have to drive a car to get somewhere, you stop to think if it's worth the trouble, and a lot of the time you don't go. You can call people on the phone and you can talk to them in person on the phone — if the line's not busy."

Now they were ready to do a rehearsal of the final scene of the sequence inside the restaurant.

"Cast," King called out, "take your places please for the final scene in this set, beginning with Kenneth's entrance. We are not shooting. This is a blocking for camera and lights. We will play straight through, as it will appear on-screen. Everybody in place? Okay . . . ready . . . Action — Kenneth, enter!"

Through the doorway to the restaurant, an elderly, quite distinguished-looking man entered with a young blonde holding his arm. Attention turned to the table where Halcie was sitting as she reacted to the sight of the couple who had just entered. She whispered to Courtney, and Courtney announced, also sotto voce, to the others at the table, "That's the ex-husband."

The six diners turned to look at the couple as the elderly man held a chair for the blonde to sit, patting her on the arm before he, too, sat down. Their table was quite a distance from where Halcie and her five embarrassed com-

170

panions sat. It was obvious that the ex-husband hadn't spotted her. Zoe said to Halcie, "Your ex-husband, huh? Small world!"

"Yes," Halcie said, and lifted her napkin from her lap and placed it on the table. "I think perhaps I'd like to leave, if you will all excuse me."

"Hold it! Hold it!" Zoe said, waving Halcie back into her chair.

Zoe got up, and slowly made her way through the tables, her eye on a waiter carrying a full tray of glasses of water as he approached the table where the couple sat. She and the waiter reached the table at the same time. Pretending she didn't see the waiter, Zoe tried to squeeze between the tables, and as if accidentally, she bumped his arm and the water glasses toppled over on the tray, drenching the couple at the table.

The blonde stalked out of the restaurant and the elderly man hurried after her.

Zoe went back to her own table. She dusted her hands together and said, "Well, that's taken care of. Shall we dine?"

Halcie, laughing, threw Zoe a kiss.

"Beautiful!" King called out. "That's all for today. Tomorrow we shoot the scene. Have a good night."

Halcie hugged Courtney and Zoe, said a few

words to the other actors in the scene, and started toward the door to go home when she noticed someone waving to her and calling her name. When she got closer she saw, to her surprise, that it was Lieutenant Staver, leaning against the wall near the entrance.

He came forward to greet her and they shook hands.

"Lieutenant," she said, "what brings you here?"

"You," he said smiling. "I need another favor."

He could see that she was immediately interested.

He told her what he wanted, an opportunity to get together, informally, with most of the members of the production company.

"You mean," Halcie said, delighted, "gathering all the suspects together, as in an Agatha Christie mystery, so you can eliminate them one by one and then announce the identity of the killer?"

Staver laughed. "Not exactly that, no."

As he had expected, she knew precisely how to arrange what he wanted.

FADE IN — Airlines terminal LAX. Late afternoon — Peggy and Elizabeth are there to see Suzie off to New York. They are —

Edgell stopped typing the script, read over what he had written, and got up from the desk and walked over to the window. Down below the ocean was calm. The sun was setting and the sky was a dark violet color.

The scene he was trying to write was the last one in *Misplaced Affection*, and it wasn't working the way he wanted.

He liked the idea of closing the film with a scene at the L.A. airport to create a unity with the opening scene at JFK Airport in New York. He was satisfied that the reason the three were there was because Peggy, played by Courtney, and Elizabeth, played by Halcie, were saying goodbye to Suzie, played by Zoe, who in the film was returning to New York after her plans to marry in L.A. had fallen through.

Still, the scene needed another element, and he hadn't been able to create it. He'd been working on the scene for almost a week, while in between he did minor revisions on the rest of the script. Usually, when he was stuck on a plot point, as he was now, his subconscious came up with a solution.

He went back to the desk and sat down. He read over the words he'd typed and sat thinking until the phone rang. It was Jack King.

"Hello, Writer. How's it going?"

"Jack, how are you? Any problems at the studio?"

"No," King said. "We had a good day of shooting, picked up another half day on the schedule."

"Good," Edgell said. "I finished most of the revisions and have the new pages to be Xeroxed."

"I'll tell Maggie. She'll call you and send somebody to pick them up. How about the ending?"

"It's in the word processor now," Edgell said. "And since I have most of the revisions out of the way, I hope to finish it in the next few days."

"Fine." King said. "Listen, Writer, the real purpose of my call is to invite you to my place on Saturday. A barbecue. I'm asking everyone on the picture — give us a chance to schmooze. You'll be there?"

"Sure. Sounds like fun. And I can use a break. Is everyone coming?"

King laughed. "What you want to know is, is Courtney coming? Yeah. And so's everyone else. Try to get there about noon."

"I'll be there," Edgell said.

10

On Saturday morning Staver carefully followed the directions King had given him to his house in the Valley. At exactly 11:45 A.M. he drove through the redwood gateposts that stood at the entrance to a long, winding drive. A small metal sign embedded in one of them read KING, so he knew he was at the right place.

Past the gateposts, tall, bushy hedges grew on either side of the drive, which ran on for a half mile with no sight of the house or grounds. Then the drive curved one final time and there was a stone fence, stone gateposts, and beyond them a sweep of green lawn and an imposing Colonial-style house. The surface of the driveway turned from black asphalt to white gravel.

As Staver followed the circular drive, he could see that, in back, there was a swimming pool, tennis courts, and a stable. Several large dogs approached the car as he stopped at the front portico, and an elderly man called out,

"The dogs won't bother you. Mr. King's around in back with some of the others." He pointed. "You can park right over there."

Staver moved the car to one side of the gravel drive where several other cars were already parked and got out. The man walked over, the dogs close to him, obedient. Staver said, "I'm John Staver. I think Mr. King is expecting me."

"Yes, sir, Mr. Staver. I'm Luis. I work for Mr. King."

Luis was tall, gray-haired and dark-skinned — Mexican probably, Staver judged — and perhaps in his mid-fifties, which was not quite as old as he had appeared to be at first glance. "They'll be expecting you," he said. "You can just walk around the side of the house. You'll see them in back."

"Thanks."

There were sprinklers twirling here and there on the lawn and a smell of fresh-cut grass in the air. Flowers grew along the borders between the gravel drive and the lawn. As Staver rounded the side of the house, he could see dense woods grew behind, and on either side, a semicircular living wall enclosing house and land behind the man-made stone wall in front. The well-tended grounds had been hewn out of the wild-growing woods where, Staver thought, there were probably still deer and perhaps even coyotes and where there had once been cougars.

In back of the house there were about a dozen people sitting in deck chairs around the swimming pool. Close by was a long bar with a white cloth draped over it and covered by an awning extending from the eaves at the rear of the house. A bartender in a white coat was serving. Farther down on the lawn was an extended table, chairs arranged around it, beneath another awning set up on tent poles.

King got up from one of the chairs around the swimming pool and went to greet Staver.

"Lieutenant, glad you could join us."

"Thank you." Staver looked around. "Quite a spread you have here."

"I moved here thirty years ago," King said. "It's only taken me from then to now to get it the way it looks today. What'll you have to drink?"

"A Bloody Mary would do nicely."

He stood waiting while King went to the bar. He recognized some of the people around the pool: Halcie Harper, Joan Strickland, and Maggie Geneen. He thought one of the men was the screenwriter James Edgell. The others were strangers to him.

King came back with the drink, then took him over to where the others sat and introduced him. He explained that several of the

177

people present were members of the crew on the new Strickland Productions film, *Misplaced Affection*.

Halcie tried to make Staver comfortable by telling the others that he was her date for the day.

Staver recognized by name one of the men who was a stranger to him: Marty Cowell. He remembered hearing that there was some kind of trouble between Cowell and Strickland at one time and that later, at Strickland's party the night before he was murdered, Cowell had shown up with Joan Strickland and there was an incident that had been reported in Didi Jones's column.

Joan Strickland's remark, in a loud voice after King had finished introducing Staver, was: "It looks to me like more than the barbecue is going to be grilled today."

Halcie was entertaining the others with a story about her early days in Hollywood.

"When I had my first screen test," she said, "the director and the cameraman decided that only the left side of my face was photogenic, and that I would always be seen by movie audiences only from that side. It was unsettling to me that I was to have only half a face. For all my scenes in the films I made, the sets had to be constructed so they could photograph me from the left. And of course that meant audiences saw only the right sides of the faces of my leading men, including Gary Cooper, Clark Gable, and Ronald Colman. That actually happened, and nobody noticed it!"

Then King told of a sneak preview he had gone to the night before of a new film, *O.K. in L.A.*, which was being released by Centurion Studios. "A mumble movie," he called it. "You couldn't hear a damn word of the dialogue, and every movement of the actors looked like it'd been shot in time lapses."

King added that afterward Denny Thompson, who'd produced the film, asked him what he thought of it. "What could I tell him? I couldn't say that I thought the only way anyone would watch it was if subtitles were added and people played it on their videocassettes at fast-forward speed."

Staver was enjoying himself so much, sipping Bloody Marys, listening to the stories about the movie business, that he almost forgot his purpose in being at the barbecue.

Other guests had arrived: Courtney, Eddie McCoy, Herman Wolfe, the production company's chief counsel, and his wife, and Henry Bickle, who had been Arthur Strickland's personal lawyer and now apparently was

Joan's. Bickle's wife was with him.

The last guest to appear was Willard Hill, an old character actor whose movies made twenty or thirty years earlier Staver still saw on TV from time to time. King explained that Hill was in the new film, playing the role of Halcie's ex-husband.

Once Hill was there, King led them to the chairs and table under the awning.

He explained to Staver that Maria, the housekeeper-cook, who was filling the table high with food, was Luis's wife and that the Mexican couple had taken care of him for a long time. "Through five wives," King said, laughing. "And a few lady friends."

On the table were great platters of beef ribs, cole slaw, onion rings, French fries, potato salad, corn bread, mounds of butter, green salad, and pitchers of wine, beer, and Bloody Marys.

At one point during the meal, when there was a silence at the table, Bickle called to Staver in a loud voice, "I wonder, Lieutenant, I'm sure we're all curious, has there been any progress in your investigation?"

Staver saw that everyone at the table was staring at him, waiting for an answer. He had anticipated he would be asked the question sooner or later that day.

"There's a person we've been looking for," he told them. "An unidentified woman who somehow managed to slip into the auditorium the night of the Oscars."

He took from his jacket pocket one of the photographs he had had made from the videotape of the woman, and passed it around the table. "Do any of you know her? Does she look familiar?"

Each of the people looked at the photograph. No one said they knew or even remembered seeing the woman. Staver took the photograph back and returned it to his pocket. He hadn't found out anything about the woman, but he *had* diverted them all away from Bickle's question.

"Do you think it's possible the murder might not ever be solved?" Edgell asked.

Staver glanced at him. "No. I think we'll solve it all right. In time."

The two of them were walking along a path in the woods behind King's house. After lunch the group had separated, some going for a horseback ride, some for a swim in the pool, others to play tennis. Halcie was reading a novel, and King, Henry Bickle, Eddie McCoy, Marty Cowell, and Willard Hill were playing high-stakes gin rummy at the table under the awning. Staver had wanted to take a walk, and Edgell had joined him.

Edgell picked up a small stone from the ground. "You know what I think?" he said.

Staver glanced at him again. "What's that?"

"I think you suspect one of us here today killed Arthur."

"And what makes you think that?" Staver asked.

Edgell was looking at the stone in his hand. "The fact that you're here. It's a logical assumption, I would say."

"Until we find out who the murderer is," Staver said, "there are a lot of *possible* suspects. Mostly what I'm interesting in is finding out as much as I can about a man who was killed, a man who was a complete stranger to me. And, yes, it's true that most of the people here today know a whole lot more about him than I do."

"And some may even have had a motive for killing him." Edgell held up the stone between two fingers and studied it. "I think this is an Indian arrowhead. Jack says they wash up out of the ground around here once in a while."

Staver couldn't tell, from the shape of the stone, what it was, but he didn't say anything.

Edgell said, "I suppose by now you've heard stories or rumors that I wasn't too happy that

Arthur didn't want Courtney and me going together."

Staver hadn't heard that. He kept walking, waiting for Edgell to continue.

They walked on side by side for a few more paces until Edgell finally said, "Well, I didn't kill him. And I don't know who did. I wanted you to know those facts."

Staver noticed that Edgell had started to sweat slightly, a thin sheen of perspiration above his upper lip. He saw that he was waiting for a response to the statement he had just made. What Staver said was: "Duly noted, Mr. Edgell."

"Hi!" Zoe said, plopping into the deck chair next to the one where Staver was sitting alone, smoking a cigarette.

She had just come out of the pool and had a giant towel draped around her shoulders. She dabbed at the beads of water sprinkled across her face and vigorously rubbed her short hair with the towel. Her body, a golden tan, glistened under a sheen of suntan lotion and water between the narrow strips of her brief bikini.

She finished drying herself off and turned sideways in the chair to face him.

"Well now," she said mischievously, "you

know, don't you, that almost everyone here" — she waved a hand around in the air — "is intimidated by your presence? I mean, I think everyone here expects you to suddenly stand up and announce that you've solved the murder and the reason you're here is to reveal the name of the killer and that then you're going to drag him, or her, away to jail."

Staver laughed and shook his head. "I wish it were that easy. No, it's highly unlikely I'll be able to do that today."

"Let's play detective," she said, looking around the grounds and making a game of it. "Who are the most likely suspects?" She turned back to him.

He said, "Why don't you tell me?"

"The wife?" she asked, looking toward Joan sitting at the pool talking to Maggie. "She had the most to gain." She shifted her view to Marty Cowell playing gin at the table. "Maybe Marty, her boyfriend — as he appears to be? Surely a suspect, wouldn't you say?"

Staver laughed. "You're the detective; I'm only a guest here."

"All right." She caught her lower lip between her teeth. "The two lawyers, then? With Arthur dead, who knows how much *they* may have gotten away with of Arthur's hidden assets that nobody else but them ever knew about! If I were a detective I surely wouldn't eliminate them."

She paused and looked back at Joan and Maggie, who were still talking together. "Strickland's secret mistress, who everybody in the world expected Arthur would marry, Maggie Geneen?"

Staver shook his head. "If I were the DA, I'd have to say your case there is the weakest one so far. I should think she'd have the most to *lose*."

Zoe looked at Courtney, who was swimming in the pool. "Then there's Courtney. They say Arthur caused her husband's suicide. Or, if that's not motive enough, that Arthur broke up her affair with Jim Edgell. How about her? Or for that matter, how about Jim himself? Certainly, it seems to me that both qualify as likely suspects. How am I doing?"

"Not bad," Staver said. "But there's one problem with some of your suspects. Whoever killed Arthur Strickland had to have been at the Oscar Awards. Some of the ones you've suggested were there, but not all of them."

"In that case," Zoe said, "we can add some more to the list." She looked around the grounds again. "Halcie, Jack — oh, hey, Eddie! Eddie McCoy, he was there. Maybe he did it — for the publicity." She looked at

185

him again. "Me," she said, "I could be a suspect; I was at the Awards."

Here it is, Staver thought, the real reason she wanted to play the game, to talk to him: She, like Edgell, wanted to get some kind of statement on the record with him. He decided to play along with her.

"You were at the Awards, all right," he said, "but you haven't established a motive for yourself, as you did with the other suspects."

She looked at him searchingly, now serious. "Some people, a few people, might have thought Arthur was developing a crush on me."

Staver turned his attention to lighting another cigarette as he asked, "And was he?"

"He liked me, yes," Zoe said, straightforward. "But that's all it could ever have been. He knew that."

Staver, speaking very carefully, said, "I want to ask you, and I — please, don't discuss this with anyone else: Did Maggie know that Strickland was — as you put it — developing a crush on you?"

"Oh, gosh, no!" Zoe blurted out. "At least, I don't think so. You don't believe —"

Staver cut he off. "I don't believe anything, necessarily. It was just a question in passing."

Zoe was silent then, thinking.

Staver wanted to cheer her up. "You know

what I think about you, Miss Rushell?"

"Zoe," she said. "Call me Zoe."

"You know what I think about you, Zoe?" he said. "I think you'd make a helluva good detective."

She smiled in delight. She said, again mischievously, "Oh, in that case, I have one more suspect to add to the list."

"And who might that be, Zoe?"

"Geoffrey, Arthur's houseman, of course." She laughed. "The butler did it."

Maggie Geneen wore the large sunglasses with the dark opaque lenses she had worn the last time Staver saw her, at Strickland's house when he'd picked up the anonymous threatening letters. He realized he had never seen her eyes.

He had gone over to the swimming pool to talk to her after Joan left poolside and went down to the stables to join some of the members of the film crew who had returned from a horseback ride.

Maggie was wearing a loose-fitting sundress and a straw hat with a wide brim. The dress concealed her figure and the hat and sunglasses concealed most of her face. She sat in a reclining position in the deck chair and didn't look at him while they talked.

He told her that it was good to see her again and thanked her for helping him recover Strickland's letters. She asked if he thought they were a clue, and he told her it was too early yet to know how important they might prove to be.

When she asked him what the police were doing to try to locate the unidentified woman, he told her that copies of the photographs he had shown them had been circulated throughout the L.A. Police Department. He added that several patrolmen reported they believed they had seen the woman at various points around the city. If the individual they saw was the woman in the photograph, she was most likely a bag lady living on the streets. They were on the lookout for her.

Maggie shook her head wearily and said it was all like a nightmare, and what was particularly terrible was not knowing who the murderer might be. Speaking slowly, she went on to explain that she frequently and suddenly found herself, in the midst of whatever she was doing, believing for a moment that this person or that person was the one who killed Arthur, people she saw every day, even worked with every day.

"And the worst thing," she said softly, "is that I'm sure this person or that person, people I have suspected, are probably wondering the same about me: Did *I* do it?"

"Well, Lieutenant," Halcie put her book across her lap as Staver approached, "have you made any progress today?"

He sat in the chair next to her and lit a cigarette. "Hard to tell," he said.

She looked at him. "Was it worth it? The trip out here?"

"Oh, that's for sure. And I'm grateful to you for arranging it." He started to say something else, then paused as he noticed Edgell and Courtney at the bar having what appeared to be an argument. He couldn't hear what they were saying, but he could see Edgell walk away from Courtney, then turn and walk back; and the two of them would talk and Courtney would walk away, and Edgell would go after her and catch her arm, and they'd talk again briefly. Finally, Courtney walked away quickly and went over and spoke to King at the gin table. Edgell stayed at the bar and the bartender fixed him a drink.

"I wonder what that was all about," Halcie said.

Staver didn't have time to answer because Courtney was coming toward them.

"I have to run now," Courtney said, leaning and kissing Halcie on the cheek.

189

"It was so good to see you, dear," Halcie said.

Courtney stuck out her hand to Staver, who was now standing. "Lieutenant, good luck with your investigation."

"Thank you, Miss Ware."

"I had hoped we might talk," Courtney said to him. She held his hand tightly.

"Perhaps another time," he said.

She smiled at Halcie and Staver and walked away. Staver watched her go around the side of the house, not stopping to speak to Edgell, who was drinking at the bar.

Staver sat down again in the chair next to Halcie. "She certainly is a beautiful lady."

"Yes, she is," Halcie agreed. "And with all the fame and success she's had so recently, it hasn't been an easy time for her."

"Do you know what their relationship is now?" Staver asked. "Hers and Edgell's, I mean."

"No. No, I don't."

Maria, King's housekeeper, came out onto the back lawn carrying a cordless phone, and went to the table where King was playing gin. King took the phone and came over to Halcie and Staver.

"It's for you, Lieutenant," King said, holding the phone out to Staver.

Staver moved away a few paces and, when he

noticed that everyone around was watching, turned his back as he lifted the phone to his ear. He talked for a few minutes, then returned and handed the phone to King.

"Could I have your attention, please!" Staver called out in a loud voice. He waited until most of the people who were at a distance came closer so they could hear him.

"I just received a phone call from one of my men," Staver said. "I don't have too much information yet, but they tell me they've picked up the unidentified woman in the photograph. The one we've been looking for."

He looked around at the group before he said, "They're holding her. She says she was responsible for Arthur Strickland's murder. Her name is Juliana Rawls. Does that name mean anything to any of you?"

When there was no answer, he said, "This may be a false alarm. They say she's a bag lady. That's all they know about her so far."

He shook hands with King and thanked him for the day.

When Staver had gone, King glanced around at his guests and said, "Well, let's face it: street people always did make strange bedless fellows."

Staver looked into the interrogation room

through the one-way glass window. Inside, Sergeant Murch was questioning the woman they'd brought in. A female police officer was also present.

So far all the woman would tell them was that her name was Juliana Rawls, which they had discovered from a Social Security card in her pocketbook, and that she was responsible for the murder of Arthur Strickland. She simply remained silent when Murch asked her other questions: Did she know Strickland? Why did she kill him? How did she do it without anyone seeing her? Was anyone else involved?

Staver studied her carefully through the window. She was in her thirties; her skin was a dark brown, probably from the sun, her hair needed cutting, and she wore the same long dress she had worn on the day she was videotaped at the Oscar Awards. The gardenia she had worn slightly askew in her hair that day was gone. She didn't seem worried that she had been picked up by the police, nor that she had told them she was responsible for Strickland's murder.

Ordinarily, when there was an unsolved murder that received major attention, such as Strickland's, there were always a few mentally impaired individuals, or individuals seeking publicity, who came forward and confessed. Such confessions were quickly discounted by the police, and the individuals were released.

Juliana Rawls would have seemed to be just such a person, except that when she was first brought into the precinct, the police had tricked her into printing by hand her name, age, and date of birth — all that she was willing to give them. Her hand-printed words were then turned over to the department's handwriting experts, who, after a comparison with the printing on the threatening notes to Strickland, declared she was their author.

So there was at least that connection between Juliana Rawls and Strickland, and she *had* managed to slip backstage at the Academy Awards and could have, somehow, stabbed him. There was no choice for Staver except to consider her a prime suspect, especially after her confession.

There was, in addition, one other element Staver had to consider: He was sure that somewhere among Strickland's papers, he had seen the name Juliana Rawls. The trouble was he couldn't recall exactly where. The other members of the task force were busy at checking through the boxes of papers.

The woman had been carrying two shopping bags and a suitcase when the police picked her up. The precinct property clerk had logged in the contents of the shopping bags and suitcases. Now Staver, turning away from the window in the interrogation room, began to inspect the few pitiful objects she had had in her possession: Two unopened cans of condensed milk. A withered orange. A four-day-old newspaper. A pair of scuffed and worn shoes. A cloth coat. A wool skirt. A length of rope. A blank postcard with a photograph of Hollywood's Walk of Fame, where the names of motion picture stars are cast in bronze. A Social Security card. A ragged wool blanket. Two crumpled one-dollar bills. One shopping bag completely stuffed with newspapers, which, Staver guessed, she used to help cover her at night when she slept in the streets. A pair of wool socks.

There was nothing among the contents to connect her with Arthur Strickland, nothing to connect her with anyone or anyplace.

Staver was returning the various articles to the shopping bags and suitcase when Detective Fried, who had been checking through the boxes of Strickland's papers, appeared in the doorway.

"You were right, Lieutenant," he said, excited. "I found a link between Strickland and the bag lady."

He handed Staver a canceled check. It was made out to Juliana Rawls in the amount of $10,000 and was signed by Arthur G. Strickland. It was dated and cashed almost a year earlier.

11

"Miss Harper, this is Lieutenant Staver."

"Good morning, Lieutenant. How are you?"

"I'm fine. Miss Harper, as you know, we're holding an individual, Juliana Rawls, for questioning in Arthur Strickland's murder."

"Yes?"

He switched the phone to his other hand. "Well, the thing is, she hasn't been willing to talk to us. But we found a check among Strickland's papers made out to her and cashed by her. The check was for ten thousand dollars. When we confronted her with it, she agreed to talk — but only if you were present."

"Me?" Halcie asked. "But I don't know her. I don't know anyone by that name."

"Well, there's no way to know why she wants to see you specifically. But it could be a great help to us it you'd come in and meet her. Would that be possible?"

"All right," Halcie said. "We're finishing up a

scene in a few minutes. I'll be there, probably in about an hour."

"I appreciate it," Staver said.

Halcie sat across the wooden table from the woman in the interrogation room. Lieutenant Staver, Detective Murch, and the policewoman were also there.

Halcie studied Juliana Rawls for a long time, both of them silent. She was positive she had never seen the woman before. Staver was standing behind Juliana Rawls. Halcie looked at him and gave a slight shake of her head. Staver shrugged.

Finally, Halcie said, "You asked to see me, dear?"

Juliana didn't answer for a moment. Instead, she smiled and reached out a hand and covered Halcie's hand outstretched on the table. There were sudden tears in her eyes as she said, "You look exactly like her, exactly like the photographs. Oh, this is so wonderful! It is just as if you were her sitting here with me."

Halcie made an attempt to smile in return. "Who am I exactly like?"

"My great-great-grandmother," Juliana said. "Her real name was Cornelia. I changed the name to Willia in the story I wrote. Somebody else changed it to Anna Rae in the movie when you played her."

Halcie was frowning. "The movie? Do you mean *The Amulet?*"

Juliana nodded. "Mr. Strickland told me that would probably happen — that they'd change the name in the movie, I mean." Her face suddenly flushed a dark red. "That was the only true thing he did tell me."

Halcie saw Staver make a motion with his hand for her to keep talking.

"You — you spoke with Arthur Strickland about the movie?" Halcie asked.

"Oh, yes." Juliana was animated as she said, "We talked a lot at the time he bought my story. He asked me all kinds of questions about my family, especially about her — Cornelia, my great-great-grandmother. But later I could never get in the studio to see him, and I called him and called him on the phone and they always said he wasn't there."

Staver had moved around from behind Juliana, and he said softly, "I'd be very angry if someone did that to me."

"Oh, I was angry all right," Juliana said. "Especially when, before he bought my story, he'd told me I'd be famous when the film was made. And then it won an Academy Award and all, and nobody even knew who I was or that it was the story I had written."

"But Mr. Strickland did buy your story, is that correct?" Staver asked, his voice still gentle.

"Of course!" Juliana looked at him, puzzled. "You saw the check. Ten thousand dollars he paid me. At that time he assured me that I was going to get more later. But I've already told you, I never talked to him again."

Staver nodded sympathetically. "But you signed a contract, didn't you?"

"Yes."

"And did it say in the contract you would receive more money?"

"It did not!" Juliana banged her fist on the table. "But he told me I would and that my name would be on the screen, and I took his word."

Staver pulled up an empty chair and sat next to her. "Didn't you have a lawyer read over the contract?"

"Mr. Strickland's lawyer did. Later, when the film came out and I saw it and knew Mr. Strickland hadn't told me the truth, I went to another lawyer."

Staver asked quickly, "Mr. Strickland's lawyer — do you remember his name?"

Juliana nodded. "Henry Bickle."

"And the lawyer you hired? What did he do?"

"Phillip Easton," Juliana said. "He went to

see Mr. Bickle, and then he told me there was nothing I could do; I had signed the contract giving Mr. Strickland the rights to the story I had written and I had been paid. That didn't seem right to me, not after what Mr. Strickland had told me."

"I see." Staver looked at her. "So what did you do then?"

"I wrote Mr. Strickland a lot of notes. I told him he was going to be punished." There were tears in her eyes. "Oh, I warned him. I was so *angry!* And when I read about the Academy Awards and that he was going to be there, I went there to kill him! He just deserved it."

Staver wanted to be very careful now that they got the whole story on the record. She had been read her Miranda rights when she was first brought in, and it was already a matter of record that she had said she understood her rights.

Staver said, "Just tell us slowly everything that happened when you went to the Academy Awards."

"Yes," Juliana drew a deep breath. "I saw Mr. Strickland go into the auditorium while I was outside with the rest of the crowd. And then I went around and slipped into one of the doors in the back of the stage. There were a lot of people around and I hid in an empty dressing room for a while, waiting for my chance."

She paused before she said, "I almost got caught. Somebody came into the dressing room and I just had time to hide behind a clothes rack so they didn't see me. They were there and left. I waited some more. Then I came out of the dressing room. I wanted him dead so much! I saw him on the stage with a lot of other people. And everything happened so quickly after that, it was like in a movie, you know, and he was dead! And I had my wish come true. I was ready to leave and — it was so odd, one of the guards saw me near the door as I was leaving. I think he thought I was coming in, and he took my arm and sort of took me outside." Her voice sounded very tired, and she stopped talking.

Staver lowered his head, frowning. He wondered if she was being deliberately vague about the moment of the stabbing so she could plead temporary insanity.

The question he asked was: "You had planned in advance how you were going to kill him?"

"Oh, yes." Juliana smiled. "All I wanted to do was get close enough to him."

"So you had the knife with you when you entered the building?" Staver asked.

"I wish I had thought of that — of a knife,"

she said, totally confusing Staver and the others in the interrogation room.

There was a silence until Halcie finally spoke. "How had you planned to kill him?"

"With a rope!" Juliana said triumphantly. "Like we'd do it back home, even though there they'd say hanging was too good for him. I was planning to get close to him, slip a noose around his neck, and choke him to death."

Staver thought he already knew the answer but he had to ask the question anyway: "What you did instead was stab him when you got close enough — is that what happened?"

She looked at him in astonishment. "No. No. *I* didn't stab him. I told you I planned to choke him to death. Somebody stabbed him before I could get close enough."

Staver sighed. He had the answer he'd expected. He said, "But you told my detectives, when they brought you in, that you were responsible for Mr. Strickland's death."

"And I am," she agreed. "I must be! I wanted it so much and I sent the notes warning him. Somebody must have picked up my vibes and done it for me, you see?"

"Then you did not stab him?"

"No."

"And you don't know who did the stabbing?"

"No."

Staver looked around the interrogation room, at Murch, at the policewoman, at Halcie. No one had a word to say.

He thought: More To Come.

Halcie didn't tell any of the others about Juliana Rawls when she returned to the studio to resume filming of *Misplaced Affection*. Lieutenant Staver had told her she was free to inform them that the woman did not kill Arthur Strickland — the story would be released to the media, anyway — but she discovered there were already problems on the set. She didn't want to add a further distraction.

The scene they were shooting was the interior of a large modern apartment in Los Angeles. In the film the characters portrayed by Courtney and Halcie are sharing the apartment. Halcie was not in the particular scene they were filming, and she stood on the sidelines, watching.

In the scene Courtney is alone in the apartment when the character of Halcie's ex-husband, played by Willard Hill, appears.

Halcie watched as the cameras rolled.

The door buzzer sounded and Courtney went to the door, opened it and, after an appropriate awkward pause, said, "Oh, I didn't recognize you at first. Elizabeth is out, I'm afraid."

"May I come in?" Willard asked.

"Why – uh, certainly," Courtney said.

She opened the door wider and Willard entered.

"Won't you have a seat?" she asked as she closed the door and walked back into the room.

"Cut! Cut!" Jack King called from behind the camera.

Courtney and Willard, both startled, turned toward him, in the shadows.

He came to the edge of the set. "Courtney, darling, you forgot to lock the door. Remember? Please lock the door after Willard's inside. I know it seems a minor detail. But Jim put it in the script because he thought – and I agree – that today most people *do* keep their doors locked. When you don't do it, audiences notice and, even if momentarily, register the fact. We don't want their minds to be anywhere else except up there on the screen."

"You're right," Courtney said. "I'm sorry. Let's do it again."

"Okay, let's do another take," King said.

Edgell paced back and forth near the exit door to the sound stage, anxious for the day's filming to end.

He had been working on the script that morning in Laguna when Courtney phoned him. She told him she wanted to talk to him and asked if he could pick her up at the studio in late afternoon when she finished work. He had been trying to create the ending to the film and had planned to stay in Laguna until it was done. But when she phoned, he put everything aside and drove into L.A.

During the hour he waited in the studio while she was filming, he stayed out of the way. He could see that the shooting wasn't going well, and that almost everyone on the set was growing short-tempered. Courtney kept having trouble with her actions, and then Hill began blowing his lines. King had to keep reshooting the scene. As Edgell had observed on *The Amulet,* when one of the actors in a scene began to have difficulties over and over, soon the other actors involved also began to go up in their lines or miss cues or forget bits and pieces of dialogue.

He was relieved when King shut down filming for the day and released the cast and crew. But he saw that Joan had detained Courtney. She talked to her until King intervened, giving Courtney a chance to escape.

Courtney saw Edgell waiting near the exit door. She hurried over to him and said, "Let's get out of here."

In the driveway she stopped to dismiss the car and driver assigned to her by the production company while she was working on the film, and Edgell drove them out to Malibu.

He was curious about why she had phoned him, but on the drive all she talked about was how terrible the filming had gone that day, saying it was all her fault.

"I just couldn't seem to do anything right," she said. "All my movements were wrong. I felt uncoordinated. And when I began to concentrate on where I was supposed to walk and what I was supposed to do when I got there, I began to forget my lines."

"Everyone has days like that," he said. "Didn't Halcie ever tell you about when she first started acting in the theater?"

Courtney shook her head.

Edgell laughed. "It's a funny story. She says that when she first became an actress, every time she made an entrance on stage she fell down."

"Oh, no. *Really?*"

"She says so, honest," he answered. "She says she moved too fast. To correct the problem, she took ballet lessons, but they didn't do any good, either. So you know what she did? She took boxing lessons. At the old Stillman's gym in

Manhattan. That's how she learned balance. And then she didn't fall down anymore on the stage."

"You're not making this up?" Courtney was laughing.

"No. She told that story herself. It's true."

Courtney exhaled a sigh of relief. She was still smiling. "Then I feel better."

When they were on the Pacific Coast Highway near Malibu, Edgell couldn't quite remember where Courtney's house was located — he had been there only twice before — and she had to direct him to the turnoff beach road where the white wooden split-level house stood at the far end, its back to the sand and ocean.

They went inside, and she gave him a beer and left him in the living room, saying she wanted to change clothes.

He drank the beer and wandered around the room, one whole wall of which was glass looking out on the strip of sandy beach and giving a Cinemascope view of ocean beyond.

The room was neat and tidy, the furniture modern Scandinavian pieces. There was a framed photograph of Courtney and Richard on top of a small teak table near the window, and beside the photograph was a pile of magazines and a small stack of books.

The magazines, *People, Glamour, Cosmopoli-*

tan, *The New York Times Magazine*, *Vogue*, and *Newsweek*, all had either photographs of Courtney on the cover or lines of type about stories on her inside the issues. While he was thumbing through them he heard her voice, the words inaudible, behind a closed door on the upper level of the house. At first he thought she was saying something to him, but then he decided she was talking on the telephone.

He was touched when he looked through the small stack of books, *Communion*, *Crossword Puzzle Dictionary*, *Stillwatch*, Olivier's *On Acting*, *Misery* — some old, some new, and found one of his own early novels, *The Day Before Tomorrow*, which had long been out of print. She must have found it in a secondhand section in a bookstore.

"Some of those were given to me, some I bought," she said, coming back into the living room.

"You must have bought this one," he said, showing her the copy of his book. "You never told me."

"I picked it up on one of my publicity tours. In Boston, I think," she said. "I liked it. I meant to tell you. I was proud of you."

She had changed into slacks, a tank top, and flat sandals. There was a white cashmere sweater draped around her shoulders, the long sleeves dangling by her sides. Her hair was pulled back in a chignon, a pair of sunglasses were pushed up on top of her head, and she had scrubbed all the makeup off her face.

"Let's take a walk on the beach," she said.

They went out the back of the house, across the sundeck, and down to the beach.

It was near sunset; the sky was a deep, cloudless blue, the sun a fiery ball of gold low on the horizon, and the ocean was calm, breaking in gentle waves against the shoreline.

There were other people on the beach — several couples walking slowly in both directions, some children running barefoot through the surf at the edge of the beach, an old man with a large dog on a leash. Courtney lowered her sunglasses over her eyes.

They walked for a while side by side, not talking. Edgell lit a cigarette. Courtney picked up a shell and, when they were close to the water, dropped it into the ocean.

She took a couple of quick steps forward and turned, facing him. "I'm pregnant," she said.

"Pregnant?"

"Yes. At first I wasn't sure I wanted the baby. But I've decided I do."

He was trying to think: They hadn't been together for — what? How many months?

"You see the problem, don't you?" She asked.

"The picture. We have to finish it fast. I'm three months pregnant. It's going to show soon."

For the moment Edgell didn't care about the picture. "What — what do you want to do?"

"I just told you," Courtney said. "I want us to finish the picture as quickly as possible."

Edgell reached out and put his hand on her arm. "I mean about the baby? Do you want to get married? I am responsible, aren't I?"

She shook his hand away. "I'm not talking about *that*. But no, I don't want to get married! And the baby's not your responsibility. It's mine and I'll handle it. I just don't want to mess up the picture; that's what I'm talking about."

He still couldn't get it all straight in his head. He said the only thing he could think to say: "Yes, we'll have to get the picture done as soon as we can."

She kissed him very gently. "Thanks," she whispered. She shivered suddenly and pulled the sweater closer around her shoulders. "It's chilly," she said, "I'd better go in."

They walked back to the house. Edgell's mind was full of questions, but he decided not to ask them until he'd had some time to think. She held his hand as they walked, and at the house she steered him around to where his car was parked.

"I have a hard day of shooting tomorrow," she told him, and she kissed him again and walked away toward the house.

Edgell drove slowly back along the Pacific Coast Highway to Santa Monica and circled through the town until he found a small bar on one of the side streets. He parked and went inside.

The place looked like a smaller version of the bar he'd been in with Jack King out near the airport — another neighborhood hangout, the regulars on all the stools at the bar, a few drinkers standing behind them, nobody sitting at any of the eight or nine tables in the room.

He ordered a double Jack Daniel's and water at the bar, paid for it, overtipped the bartender, and carried the drink to one of the empty tables.

He took a couple of swallows of the drink, lit a cigarette, and thought back over the scene with Courtney on the beach. Maybe he should have reacted differently to her news. But what could he have said? She hadn't told him because she wanted him to marry her or wanted money, hadn't in fact even said that he was the father. He couldn't ask her, but he had to wonder if there was someone — or had been someone — in her life since him.

He finished his drink, and the bartender asked if he wanted another. He said he did.

All Courtney wanted, he reminded himself as he drank his second Jack Daniel's, was to get the picture done in a hurry before her pregnancy began to show. A lot of money could be lost if they had to stop filming until after she had the baby. He thought about that, thought about the fact that no matter how quickly they were able to speed up filming, there was always the possibility her pregnancy would begin to show before they could finish.

Edgell had always been fascinated by how the so-called creative process — his included — operated, and that moment, when the solution to Courtney's problem came to him, was an example.

He was excited when he got up and went to the phone booth in the back of the bar and called Jack King on his private line at home.

"How are you, Writer?" King said, recognizing his voice.

"Fine, Jack. Listen," Edgell said, talking quickly, "I've got the ending to the movie. In that last scene, at the airport, when the three women, Halcie, Courtney, and Zoe get together to say good-bye, Courtney tells the other two" — Edgell paused — "she's pregnant! She's pregnant by her dead husband. They're all thrilled, end of movie."

"I think," King said slowly, "it's a stroke of genius."

"In the scenes leading up to the ending," Edgell said, "you can add some weight to her, subtly. None of the other characters in the film comment on it, but at the end the audience will wonder why they didn't put two and two together and figure it out for themselves. What do you think?"

"I like it, Writer. I like it."

"Then that's the way we do it?"

"That's the way we do it," King said.

Edgell dialed Courtney's number but did not leave a message when her answering machine came on the line. Served him right, he thought, for having written that speech in the film for Zoe about answering machines.

12

They were playing poker, the seven of them in the Homicide Task Force — John Staver, Frank Murch, Will Tolbin, Andy Tomasini, Pete Ardis, Morrie Fried, and Ed Cooney — in Staver's apartment.

Staver had always thought it was a good idea to get the men together once in a while away from the office, that it made them a closer-knit unit. Sometimes the seven of them went out for a Chinese or Mexican dinner or for an evening of drinking. Tonight he'd invited them to play poker at his place.

"I got to tell you this story about yesterday, why I was late getting to work," Cooney, who was dealing, said.

He shuffled the cards. "Yesterday morning I'm upstairs getting dressed and the wife calls up to me frantically and says the kid's missed the school bus. I got to take her to school right away, the missus says, or she'll be marked tardy."

He began dealing the cards around. "Arlene's very touchy these days what with the new baby coming, so I know I got to take the kid *right away* if Arlene says *right away*. So even though I'm about half dressed, I put on my raincoat, run downstairs, grab Janie, and drive her to her school. I get her there on time, and there I am in the car, wearing a shirt, a tie, shoes and socks, and a raincoat. I see it's late so I decide not to go back home. Arlene always heads for the living room sofa to sleep in the morning as soon as the kid's out of the house anyway."

He finished dealing the hand. "The dry cleaner we use is only a block away from Janie's school and I remember I got a suit in there ready to be picked up. Also, I had taken time to shove my wallet and badge in the raincoat pocket, and my gun and harness are at the precinct. So I stop at the dry cleaner, put on the suit that's ready, and go on to work."

He paused, laughed, and said, "A couple of hours after I'm at the precinct, Arlene calls, all frantic again. She's awakened and seen my pants and jacket I was going to wear still lying on the bed. She wants to know what I'm wearing. I tell her I'm assigned to desk duty and I'm still wearing my raincoat. And last night when I checked out, I took off the suit, put it back in the dry cleaning-bag, and wore my raincoat home. I never say a word of complaint about being rousted out of the house that morning. Man, was Arlene contrite and nice as pie all last evening."

They all laughed at Cooney's story.

Staver folded his poker hand and went to the kitchen to get more beers all around. He had been divorced for one year, but since he had been married for only one year it hadn't been that difficult to make the adjustment back to being single again. He and his ex-wife, Celia, were still friends and had lunch together once in a while, even though she'd left him to marry a vice president in the bank where she'd worked as a teller. Staver didn't blame her for the breakup. The fact was they only had enough in common to sustain a lunch or a date, certainly not a marriage. He'd always thought their marriage and divorce had been about as painless as anyone could ask of both experiences.

He opened a can of beer and drank some, and thought about one of the reasons he'd wanted to have the poker game that night with the other men: he'd decided it was time for them to move forcefully, using a different approach, in the Strickland murder investigation, and he wanted to lay out the plan for them.

The media was still playing up the story.

216

Which put pressure on the Mayor who was putting pressure on the chief of detectives. Staver was feeling the heat. He could wish the media would lay off but he knew that wasn't likely to happen; there was always that blank space on newspaper pages, on the TV screen, on the radio airwaves, to be filled. The Strickland murder was made to order for the media.

Their most promising lead had seemed to be the apprehension and identification of the unknown woman, the bag lady. Now they knew her story checked out; Staver had had the two lawyers involved, Henry Bickle and Phillip Easton, brought in for interrogation.

Bickle readily admitted that Strickland had indeed bought the film rights to the story of *The Amulet* from Juliana Rawls. Bickle had drawn up the contract; Juliana Rawls had read it and signed it and been paid ten thousand dollars.

When Staver pressed him on whether he thought the contract was fair to Juliana Rawls, he shrugged. It was a business deal, he answered; *he* hadn't made it, his client had. Besides, he added, in the majority of cases in the motion picture business when a producer was interested in a story property, the deal was made for option money only and was, more often than not, for considerably less than ten thousand dollars. He claimed he was not present at any discussion Strickland might have had with Juliana Rawls about future monies or credits. Nor, he said, was he aware of any such verbal discussions about which they had only her word.

Easton was no more forthcoming about his involvement in the matter. He claimed that by the time Juliana Rawls came to see him and he went to talk to Bickle, the picture had been made, and Strickland had a legally signed contract for all movie rights in the story and had paid for them. He, too, pointed out to Staver that Strickland, as a businessman, had naturally made the best possible deal for himself, as far as he, Easton, was concerned. Of course Juliana Rawls could have sued Strickland, Easton added; he had pointed out that possible course of action to her, while at the same time reminding her it could cost her a fortune, which she didn't have.

As Staver concluded his interrogation of Bickle and Easton, he remembered a quotation he had heard when he was taking a course in criminal justice at UCLA for his lieutenancy exam: "God save us from a lawyer's et cetera." But there wasn't much he could do about his feelings except to curtly dismiss the two, for the present at least.

With Juliana Rawls no longer a possible suspect, Staver knew he had to change the direction of the investigation.

He gathered up an armful of beer cans from the refrigerator and went back to the poker table. He figured the time had come to put real heat on all the people who had been close to Strickland, and he knew exactly how to do it.

Joan Strickland's dinner party that night had had to be arranged on short notice; Raymond Caudell had flown in from New York in the morning and announced to Stephan Rogin, president of Centurion Studios, that he wanted to meet at dinner with all the principal people filming *Misplaced Affection*.

Arthur G. Strickland Productions, as it was still called, was co-producing *Misplaced Affection* with Centurion Studios. Caudell was executive vice president of Jower-Ex, the conglomerate that owned Centurion Studios, and was chairman of Centurion. When Rogin informed Joan that Caudell wanted the dinner meeting, she decided to hostess the affair. Better, she reasoned, to have Caudell on her turf.

On the guest list were Caudell and his wife, Sheila, and Rogin and his wife, Adele. Then she didn't invite, but commanded, Halcie Harper, Courtney Ware, Jack King, Jim

Edgell, Zoe Rushell, Eddie McCoy, and Herman Wolfe and his wife, Polly, to attend the dinner.

Joan was out of the studio for the rest of the day after she received the phone call from Rogin. She hired an extra cook, two butlers, and a serving maid, and sent Geoffrey, the houseman, off to do the shopping for the menu she had planned. She spent almost as much time that afternoon working out the seating arrangements as she had supervising the preparation of the meal. She placed Caudell between Halcie and Courtney to one side of the center of the table. Sheila Caudell sat directly opposite her husband between Jack King and Jim Edgell. Zoe Rushell and Herman Wolfe were seated next to Edgell toward the far end of the table on one side, and Eddie McCoy and Polly Wolfe on the other. Joan placed herself in the seat Arthur had always occupied, at the head of the table, with Rogin to her right, his wife to her left. Marty Cowell occupied the chair at the foot of the table.

Caudell, as was expected, dominated most of the dinner conversation. "Sheila and I are honored to be here," he announced, raising his wine glass in the motion of a toast, "rubbing elbows with the four most distinguished members of the filmmaking community, as was agreed by your peers this year." He aimed his glass at one, then another, as he said, "Halcyon Harper, Courtney Ware, Jack King, Jim Edgell, I salute your talent."

He went on to say that he expected another dinner party next year, when he would drink a toast to all of them now making *Misplaced Affection.* He added that he thought they might have some competition from the new picture, *Manhattan Townhouse,* just released by Centurion.

He looked around the table. "Have you seen the reviews on it the last few days? *Time, The New Yorker, New York* magazine, all the dailies – big-city, small-town – Shalit, Siskel and Ebert, Christ, Liz Smith, Sarris – all raves." He expounded on the talents of the writer-director of *Manhattan Townhouse.*

King, having passed up the wine in favor of more Chivas Regal, sipped his scotch and listened to Caudell continue to praise the genius behind the new film. King had heard it all before. This particular writer-director made off-beat *auteur* movies on a modest budget that made a modest profit, or no profit, but that always got rave reviews. The genius writer-director was spared the squeeze the studio brass put on most moviemakers to come up with a box office blockbuster. King understood well enough that the man Caudell was lauding was Centurion Studio's token *cinéma artiste* to be trotted out and displayed whenever there was a public outcry of excessive sex and violence in the studio's other movies.

Toward the end of the dinner, Caudell finally got around to the subject that was the real purpose of his visit. He said he was concerned by all the media publicity about Juliana Rawls, now that she had been released by the police but was still claiming she had written the story of *The Amulet*. What he wanted to know was if this was going to adversely affect Arthur G. Strickland Productions and hurt the box office chances for *Misplaced Affection*.

Joan quickly answered that the matter had been resolved. She had authorized payment of one hundred thousand dollars to the woman for the rights to the story and given her 2 percent of the film's gross, which was within the Screenwriters Guild contract guidelines. In addition, she had had new prints of the film made, crediting the original story to Rawls.

"There's no chance of any sort of lawsuit against AGS Productions, then?" Caudell asked.

"Herman," Joan said, looking down the table, "your turn."

"She gave us a signed letter of agreement to

that effect," Wolfe said. "She's back home in Arizona."

"Good!" Caudell nodded. "Now, according to the daily production reports I've been receiving on *Loving Kindness* in New York, you're six days behind schedule. Are we going to be able to make that up?"

This time Joan looked at King. "Jack, you want to give us your estimate?"

"By the time we wind up," King told them, looking around the table, "I think I can safely say we'll meet the original schedule."

Joan spoke up. "As extra insurance that we'll bring the picture in on time, I've appointed — and this is the first time the cast and crew will have heard — Marty Cowell to serve as producer of *Misplaced Affection*. I will of course remain as executive producer."

She gave Caudell a big smile as she added, "I'm sure you're aware of Marty's reputation as a producer of quality films."

Caudell nodded, smiling. Joan raised her wine glass in a toast to Cowell, and he in return raised his.

King leaned over to whisper to Edgell, "Yeah. It's word of mouth that kills his pictures at the box office."

Sheila Caudell, who overheard King's remark, almost choked as she tried to smother her laughter.

Caudell said his final question was: Did anyone know how the police investigation into Arthur's murder was progressing?

"I understand they're still actively working on the case," Joan said. "More than that I don't think anyone knows."

"But surely they don't think anyone who was close to Arthur committed the murder?" Caudell asked, frowning. "Do they?"

"Well," Joan said slowly, "they've questioned almost everyone who knew him. But I'm told that's normal procedure in any such case."

"Yes, it is," Wolfe said quickly, nodding at Caudell. "It's routine."

Caudell started to say something, then changed his mind. "A most unfortunate affair," he said instead.

When they finished dessert, Joan served after-dinner drinks in the library, where Caudell was, as Joan had anticipated, properly impressed with the Picassos, Mirós, and Matisses hanging on the walls.

King, sipping brandy, called Halcie's attention to Caudell, Joan, and Cowell huddling together at the opposite end of the library.

"I'll bet," King said, "Arthur must be turning over in his urn."

13

"Miss Geneen! Miss Geneen! Wait up."

Maggie turned on the sidewalk.

Staver took a couple of steps closer to her and said, "What a coincidence. I was just passing, and I thought I recognized you when you came out of that health club back there."

"Yes, you recognized me, Lieutenant," Maggie said, thinking that the meeting was no coincidence. He must have been waiting for her outside the health club, which meant he must have followed her there from her apartment. So she was being watched. What did that mean?

"Well, now that we've run into each other," Staver said with a smile, "perhaps we can talk again, if it won't inconvenience you."

"I'm just going to stroll back to my apartment," Maggie said. "You're welcome to join me."

Her apartment was approximately a mile away. Staver fell into stride beside her as she set off to walk the distance.

He lit a cigarette. "You work out every day?"

"If I can find the time." She turned her head to look at him. "You really shouldn't smoke, Lieutenant."

"I'll put it out if it bothers you."

"No, no. It doesn't bother me." She shook her head. "It's your health I was thinking of."

"You're absolutely right," he said. "It's just that it's awfully hard to *un*teach an old dog old tricks."

Maggie had to laugh. "I suppose — when you put it that way."

He looked at her more closely. "Do you have a streak there — something on the lens of your glasses? The right lens?"

They both stopped while she took off her sunglasses, held them up and, even though she didn't see anything on the lenses, wiped the glasses off with a tissue she removed from a pocket in her slacks.

Staver saw her eyes for the first time. They were green with flecks of gold, and he was startled by the effect they had on him, as if he were seeing her somehow physically different, more feminine, more — sensual, he felt, than his previous impressions of her.

She put her sunglasses back on and they resumed their walk.

Maggie said, "You mentioned that perhaps we could talk again. What did you want to say?"

"As you may have guessed" — Staver flipped his cigarette away — "we still have questions about Arthur Strickland's death."

"Yes?"

He glanced at her. "Now that we've discovered who was writing him the notes and eliminated her — Juliana Rawls — as a possible suspect, well, we're back to square one. And the videotapes made the night of the Oscars are about all we have to go on. So far they haven't told us what we want to know. Have you ever seen the tapes?"

Maggie continued to look straight ahead. "No, I'm afraid I haven't. And I don't think I'd care to see them."

"I can understand," Staver said. "You see, what we need to do is to determine exactly where every individual was standing on the stage at the moment Mr. Strickland was stabbed."

"And the tapes don't show you that, I assume?"

Staver was still looking at her as they walked. "Not exactly, no. For instance" — he made the remark sound conversational — "we don't know exactly where you were at the time."

She stopped walking suddenly and turned to face him. "Me? I wasn't even on the stage. Surely whatever videotapes you have show that. I was still in the audience."

"Ah, now you see the problem?" he asked. "The tapes don't show you on the stage, that's the problem. Because if they did, and you were nowhere near him, well, that would be that. The thing is that of course the tapes also don't show much of the audience, so we can't place you there, either. Incidentally, what I'm saying about what the tapes do and don't show of you is true of the other people who were, well, a part of Arthur Strickland's life."

Maggie had pushed her sunglasses up, as if to see him more clearly, and she was frowning. "I guess I'm not following you. If the tapes don't show me on stage, obviously —"

Staver raised a hand, interrupting her. "We have reason to suspect that the person who stabbed Mr. Strickland was wearing a disguise."

"I see." Maggie nodded slowly. "Now I do follow you. So the tapes can reveal, to a degree, who *didn't* do it, but not, of the people who might have had access to the stage, who *did* do it."

"Exactly." He took her arm and they started walking again. "Please believe, I'm not accusing you. I just want you to know the situation.

228

And I will be having this same conversation with others."

"Somebody must have seen me in the audience at the time Arthur was stabbed," Maggie said. "I'll have to think about who might have noticed me there."

"If you find them, please let me know."

"That's what you call having an alibi, isn't it?" She still had her sunglasses pushed up.

Staver looked into her green eyes and wondered about the first time Arthur Strickland must have looked into those eyes and seen, felt, her sensuality, as he himself had today.

"That's what you call having an alibi," he told her.

Eddie McCoy had just finished getting his hair cut in the same place in Beverly Hills he'd been going to since he was a press agent at Paramount years before. It was a barbershop then; later it was a unisex haircutting parlor; now it was a hairstyling salon. Through all the status changes of its name, and subsequent price increases, the same barber, Tony, who owned the business, had cut his hair.

It was a Saturday and Eddie had planned to play a round of golf at the Bel Air Country Club, but it had been raining since dawn. He thought about calling a couple of his friends to set up a gin game, but what he decided he really should do was go into his office at the studio and work up a couple of press releases.

He put on his jacket and raincoat and went out the door of the shop.

"Eddie McCoy, right?" said a man Eddie did not immediately recognize, who was standing on the sidewalk under the shop's awning, blocking the way.

"Lieutenant Staver," Staver said. "Remember me? The barbecue at Jack King's place? I was just passing by and I happened to glance in the window. I thought that was you inside."

Eddie buttoned the top of his coat against the rain blowing in under the awning. "How are you, Lieutenant?"

"Fine, just fine." Staver smiled. "Listen, since we've run into each other like this by accident, why don't I buy you a drink somewhere out of the rain? I've been meaning to phone you, ask you to come in so we could discuss the Strickland case again. This way we'll both save some time later."

Eddie knew damn well they hadn't run into each other by accident. Staver had to have been tailing him, which was an unnerving thought. He made a point of looking at his watch. "I guess I have time for one. I was on my way to the studio — some work

I want to get done this afternoon."

"I noticed a bar on the next block there," Staver said. "That okay?"

They hurried through the rain, not talking until they were inside the small, dark bar, which was empty except for the bartender and a man sitting on one of the stools, drinking a beer and reading a copy of the *Racing Form*.

They sat at the end of the bar and Staver paid for the two Bloody Marys they ordered.

"So what did you want to discuss?" Eddie asked.

Staver took a sip of his drink. "Well, as you know, we got sidetracked in the investigation for a while, following a false trail. Juliana Rawls and those threatening notes she wrote to Strickland. Now we're back on track."

"Good," Eddie said, "I'm glad to hear it."

"Aren't you interested to hear what we know now?"

"If you want to tell me," Eddie said, "yeah, I'd be interested."

Staver looked around the bar, looked back at Eddie. "We suspect that whoever killed him was somebody close to him, somebody who was involved in the making of the last movie, *The Amulet*."

Eddie was frowning. "What makes you suspect that?"

Staver smiled. "Let's just say for now that we know through certain information we've managed to develop."

Eddie was still frowning. "That the person was someone who actually worked on *The Amulet*?"

Staver nodded. "We have reason to think so, yeah."

"That's hard for me to believe," Eddie said slowly.

"Believe it. Tell me, you knew Strickland pretty well, wouldn't you say?"

Eddie considered his answer before he shrugged. "I knew him. How well? How well does anyone know anyone else?"

"How about his lady friends?" Staver asked quickly. "You knew about them, knew he had a reputation for liking the ladies."

Eddie smiled. "I like the ladies myself, Lieutenant. What does that tell you? It's a heterosexual hazard, wouldn't you say?"

Staver laughed out loud and held up a hand. "Okay, okay." He added, "But there's a difference between you and Strickland: He liked the ladies and somebody murdered him. It's my job to find out if there was any connection between the two things."

"I don't know what I could tell you on that score that would help." Eddie shook his head.

"Let me try to fill you in on what we're up against in trying to solve this case," Staver said, leaning forward confidentially, his voice low. "There's a man murdered who's separated from his wife but not yet divorced, whose wife it appears has a playmate. The man had a lot of lady friends, and maybe one of them didn't like it too well that he liked the others. On top of all that, he'd accumulated a more than fair share of ex-friends along the way. Any one of the above has to be considered a suspect, and anyone who was onstage or backstage at the time who can't prove where they were standing at the moment he was stabbed. You see?"

Eddie finished off his Bloody Mary. "What you seem to be saying, indirectly, Lieutenant, is you know I was backstage and you have no proof of exactly where, so I'm a suspect."

"That's about it," Staver said easily. "But of course you're not the only one. What I need is any information I can get that will help me narrow down the field."

Eddie looked at him. "And what you want from me is to see if I can come up with that kind of information."

Staver nodded. "I'd appreciate it."

"We finished here?"

"Sure thing. I know you want to get to the studio." Staver held up his half-full glass. "I think I'll finish the rest of this. See you around."

He watched Eddie go out the door into the rain.

Down the bar, Detective Tobin folded up the copy of the *Racing Form* he'd been reading and glanced over at Staver.

Staver nodded, and Tobin followed McCoy out of the bar.

Staver drank his Bloody Mary. He'd put the screws into Eddie. Now they'd see if he led them anywhere, to anyone.

Staver thought: More To Come.

Staver, in an unmarked police car, followed the station wagon when it turned off the Pacific Coast Highway onto the narrow beach road. He pulled up behind it when it came to a stop at the white wooden split-level house at the end of the road and got out of the car.

"Miss Ware," Staver called out to Courtney as she slid out from behind the steering wheel of the station wagon and stood looking at him, "I'm John Staver – Lieutenant Staver, LAPD. Remember? We met at Jack King's house."

"Yes," she said as he walked closer to her.

He smiled. "I was just passing by and I

234

thought I'd see if you were home. I have a couple of questions I'd like to ask you, if you can spare me the time."

Courtney nodded. "Yes, I suppose so." She leaned back into the station wagon and lifted out a couple of large bags of groceries. She did not appear surprised to see him.

"Here, let me help you with those," Staver said. He was carrying a manila envelope, which he stuck under his arm as he took the bags of groceries from her.

"I won't take long," he assured her as they walked toward the house. "There's something I want to show you. You do have a VCR, don't you?"

"I have a VCR, yes," she said.

"Good. This way it'll save my having to ask you to come to the precinct."

After she unlocked the door, she hesitated for a moment before she said, "Lieutenant, I wonder if you'd mind waiting for a moment until I straighten up the living room a bit. I wasn't expecting company."

"Certainly. I'll wait." He transferred the grocery bags to her and lit a cigarette after she went into the house and closed the door behind her.

The day was hot and humid in L.A., but out there at the ocean there was a cool afternoon breeze, and he could smell the salt brine of the sea a few yards away. Beds of colorful flowers grew around the front of the house. He imagined he could be very content living in a place like this.

He didn't have to wait long before Courtney opened a door again and asked him to come in.

The first thing to catch his eye in the living room was the view of the ocean outside the expanse of glass that was the fourth wall. Everything in the room, he noted, seemed to be orderly and in place.

"I'm going to have a cup of coffee," Courtney said. "Would you like a cup? Or would you rather have a drink, something stronger?"

"Coffee would be fine, thanks," he told her.

She turned and opened the door at the side of the living room. "If we're going to be using the VCR, it's in here."

He followed her into the other room, where there was a desk, chair, typewriter, file cabinets, a bookcase, a leather sofa, and a television set and videocassette recorder. The desk was piled high with newspapers, magazines, a few books, pads of paper, pencils, pens, an ashtray, and a rack of pipes in various sizes and shapes.

"I hope you'll overlook how messy this room is," Courtney said, shaking her head. "My husband, Richard, used to work in here. He was trying to write plays. I've — just never gotten around to straightening everything up, getting rid of his things." She turned away. "I'll get the coffee. It won't take but a minute."

Staver sat on the sofa. On a small end table next to it was a large photograph of Courtney and a man — he guessed it was her late husband — standing on the beach with the ocean in the background, their arms around each other's waist. Staver could see that as young as Courtney looked now, she had still subtly aged some since the picture had been taken.

He peered closely at the man, who had blond hair and a rather bland face and appeared to be a bit overweight. He briefly wondered what there was that had attracted Courtney to this man. And knew, even as he wondered, that most such speculations about what one individual saw in another, especially when applied to men and women, were nonsense.

Courtney came back into the room carrying a tray with cups, saucers, spoons, sugar, cream, and a silver coffeepot.

As she poured the coffee she told him they had finished shooting at the studio that day and she had come home early and then gone grocery shopping. He said he guessed he was lucky she had arrived back just as he stopped by. She said yes, it was and handed him a cup of coffee. He asked her if she minded if he smoked a cigarette. She said no, she didn't mind. He took a videocassette out of the manila envelope and told her it was the recording made at the Oscar ceremonies when Arthur Strickland was stabbed. He asked her if she would mind watching it with him. She told him she wouldn't mind, even though his detectives had already questioned her.

After he put the tape into the VCR he lit a cigarette, then ran the tape.

As they watched the tape, he explained to her what he thought were the important moments. First, as the scenes unrolled of the grand finale showing the crowd onstage from the front just before Strickland was stabbed, he pointed out where various individuals were standing.

"Halcie Harper helped me identify people," he told her. "Watch closely now. There's Jack King, see? Kathleen Havens behind him — look quickly! See, that's her wearing the diamond tiara behind King. There's that Indian singer — what's her name?"

"Young Rose Hightree," Courtney said.

"Now look," Staver said, "behind her. There you are. You're mostly blocked from view. Halcie spotted that ring you always wear — see it on your left hand?"

"Yes, that's me."

"And Halcie," he said, "Jim Edgell, Joan Strickland, Joyce Kimbro."

He leaned forward and stopped the tape. "Now we're going to look at the scenes taken from the rear, just after Strickland was stabbed." He pushed the Play button on the VCR.

"Watch closely," he said. "There's King bending over Strickland. And there — you see, blocking a clear view of King and Strickland lying on the stage — one of the performers in a costume, Indian dress, from *The Amulet* production number."

"I see," Courtney said.

Staver punched the Pause button on the VCR and the scene remained on the TV screen.

"Do you remember noticing that person, that performer, onstage?" he asked.

She looked at the TV screen, frowning. Finally, she shook her head. "No." She looked at Staver. "Do you think that's who stabbed Arthur?"

"I don't know. It's just that whoever it was, was standing close behind him." He didn't want to reveal to her that they knew now there was one more person onstage at the time wearing an Indian costume than there had been in *The Amulet* production number earlier.

"There's another shot I want you to see," he

said and ran the tape again, punching the Pause button when the scene showed the back of the man they'd never been able to identify, the man who was standing close to Strickland's body.

"That man there," Staver said. "Anything about him look familiar to you?"

Courtney studied the TV screen again, frowning, and again shook her head.

Staver sighed. "I was hoping, since you were in the second row, you might have noticed one or the other of those two people."

"I wish I could be of more help," she said. "There was just so much going on. Maybe if I think about it, I can recall something."

Staver pushed the button on the VCR to rewind the tape. "I still appreciate the time you've given me."

Courtney said slowly, "I did notice one person you didn't mention."

"Who?"

"Vicky Jason, Robert Jason's widow," she said. "You know."

"Yes." Staver remembered that Didi Jones had told him about Robert Jason, who had been killed in a drunken fall, and that his wife had blamed Arthur Strickland because of the way he treated Jason during the filming of *The Amulet*.

"What about her?" Staver asked.

"Just that I saw her backstage after. After Arthur was stabbed," Courtney said. "And I wondered what she was doing there."

"That's interesting," he said. "Very interesting." He took the tape out of the VCR and put it into the envelope. "It may be that you've been helpful after all."

He thanked her again for seeing him, and she walked him to the door.

He drove up the beach road toward the highway. On the police radio he called Detective Tomasini, who was parked out of sight in an unmarked car up on the bluffs above the Pacific Coast Highway, watching the entrance to the beach road from Courtney's house through binoculars.

"I'm checking out now," Staver told him. "Keep a close lookout."

"Roger," Tomasini said over the radio.

"Is this a real date or what?" Zoe asked impishly, looking at Staver.

He laughed out loud, although he himself thought it was a good question, and he didn't really know what the right answer might be. "Or what what?" he decided to answer.

"Or did you just want to — what do you police call it? — interrogate me?"

"It's not police procedure to take young ladies to dinner when they are to be interrogated," he told her.

"Then it's a real date," she said.

"It's a dinner date."

He had had a rough day, and in the late afternoon had decided he wanted some companionship at dinner. He thought of Zoe and called her on the spur of the moment at the studio. She said they were finishing up shooting and, yes, she'd like to have dinner with him. He picked a good steak place he knew on Highland Avenue. She said she had her car and she'd meet him there.

"I like it here," she said now, looking around the rustic interior of the restaurant. "It's not so California-ish, more like places back East."

They ordered steaks, baked potato, and Caesar salads, with a bottle of red wine.

Staver took a sip of the wine. "Tell me about yourself. Where are you from?"

"I grew up in Virginia, just outside Richmond," she said. She was an only child. Her father had his own advertising agency in Richmond and her mother was a music teacher at the suburban high school near where the family lived. Zoe started acting in school plays and went on to do roles in various regional theaters around the country. A director at one of the

242

theaters, in Minnesota, knew Milton Golub, the Hollywood talent agent, and gave her a letter to Golub when she went to California to appear in a small part in a play at the Mark Taper Forum. Golub took her on as a client and sent her to see Arthur Strickland, who was doing preproduction planning on *Misplaced Affection*. He signed her to a contract for the film.

"And here," she concluded, with a mock flourishing wave of her hands, "I am."

Staver smiled. "You like being an actress?"

"Sometimes I do." She looked at him. "And sometimes I think it's a completely idiotic way to spend my life. Especially being a movie actress, now that I'm experiencing it."

"Is working in films that different from working in plays?" he asked.

She nodded. "For me, at least. Film acting is too — oh, I don't know — fractured, I guess you'd call it. I can tell you it isn't much fun."

She thought for a moment and laughed. "Jack King said something funny on the set the other day about how making movies had changed over the years. He said all the problems in the movie industry, all the problems in the world, began when they stopped making tap-dancing pictures. He said that was what led to the real death of innocence in the world."

She shook her head and smiled.

Staver smiled, too. "He might just be right."

"The biggest thing I can't get used to," Zoe said, "is the way they shoot the story out of sequence all the time. For instance, we did the final scene in the film — jumped to the very end of the movie, with a whole lot yet we still had to shoot in between. You know why?"

She took a sip of wine while Staver waited.

"Jim Edgell wrote a new ending to *Misplaced Affection*," she told him. "Now, in the very last shot in the movie, when the three women who have been friends — the characters played by Courtney, Halcie, and me — say goodbye, it turns out that Courtney — the character played by Courtney — is pregnant, and it shows. That's why they wanted to film that scene now, padding her out to make her look as exactly pregnant as they wanted her to be at the end. Then little by little they will pad her figure out to match it with the last scene."

She paused when she realized that of course he didn't know what she was talking about. "I forgot to tell you the most important reason Jim wrote the new ending and why we filmed it early." She tilted her head to one side. "You see, Courtney's pregnant. In real life, I mean. We just found out ourselves. It's no secret now. But it could have wrecked the picture if Jim hadn't written it in the way he did."

244

Staver was startled by the news. "I saw Courtney a few days ago. I didn't notice."

"It hasn't really begun to show yet," Zoe said. "But when it does, now it won't make any difference in the picture."

Staver was frowning. "What's she going to do? Courtney, I mean. In real life?"

"She isn't saying."

"Didn't she and Edgell have something going for a while?"

Zoe nodded. "But everyone thinks that's ended. If he's the one, I don't think she means to marry him."

She broke into sudden laughter again. "You want to hear another remark Jack King made? When he heard the news about Courtney, he said now if it was decided to make a sequel to *Misplaced Affection*, it could legitimately be titled *The Son of Misplaced Affection*. Isn't that funny?"

"It really is," he agreed, laughing.

They finished dinner, and Staver walked Zoe out to her car in the parking lot.

He took her hand as he opened her car door. "I'd like to see you again. Okay?"

She leaned and kissed him on the cheek. "Okay," she said.

When she was in the car, he leaned in the

window. "You sure you'll be all right getting home?"

"I'll be all right," she told him. "I really enjoyed tonight. I'd like to see you again, too."

As she pulled away, he noticed a printed sign stuck on the inside of one of the car windows, the kind of sign many drivers these days put on their windows, like NO RADIO INSIDE or NO VALUABLES, to discourage break-ins when the car was parked. The printed sign inside the window of hers was: OFFICIAL MAFIA CAR.

He shook his head in amusement. He decided she'd be all right.

14

Staver let some time pass before he had Vicky Jason brought in for questioning.

What he did in the meantime was assign Detectives Ardis and Cooney to put Mrs. Jason under surveillance. They established that she had moved back into the house in Benedict Canyon where she had lived with Robert Jason until they separated shortly before his death.

After several days, Ardis and Cooney reported back that Vicky Jason led a busy social life that included many boyfriends, parties, and barhopping. They were unable to connect her, during that time, with anyone else who had known Arthur Strickland. It didn't sound to Staver as if she were shedding any tears over her departed husband, but he still decided to put her through an interrogation.

Ardis and Cooney, who picked her up and brought her to the precinct, remained in the interrogation room while Staver, after informing her of her rights, did the questioning.

"I believe you were at the Oscar ceremonies the night Arthur Strickland was stabbed?"

"Yes, I was. I was invited by a friend, actually a friend of my late husband's and mine. His name is Bernie, Bernard, Clemments. He's an assistant director on *A Man Alone,* the TV series at Centurion Studios."

"Prior to that night, hadn't you accused Arthur Strickland of causing your husband's death?"

"I may have said I didn't think he treated Robert very nicely during the filming of *The Amulet.* If that's what you mean."

"So you didn't like Strickland?"

"No. I didn't. But if you're going to ask me if I killed him, my answer's going to be the same: I didn't."

"Would you explain what you were doing backstage at the Dorothy Chandler Pavilion at the time, or directly after, Strickland was stabbed?"

"Backstage?"

"Yes, backstage."

"Who says I was backstage?"

"You were seen there."

"All right, yes, I was backstage. So were a lot of people."

"You haven't explained what you were doing there."

"All right, I'll tell you. I was leaving."

"Leaving?"

"Leaving. After the — the shock of seeing Arthur dead on the stage, I wanted to get out of there, out of the auditorium. I was sitting down in front, on the side. People behind me were blocking the way out the front entrance. I was close to the stage. I thought it would be quicker to go across the stage and out one of the exit doors in back."

"There were exit doors closer to you than that."

"I just never thought, or noticed."

"And was your escort with you in the auditorium before Strickland was stabbed?"

"No, he'd left, to get the car, before the finale."

"So no one saw you."

"You said someone saw me backstage, so someone saw me leaving."

"But that was after the stabbing."

"Which was why, I've already told you, I wanted to leave. And I left."

"And you have no idea who killed Strickland?"

"No. I only know I didn't."

"One more question: Did you ever go to,

visit, Centurion Studios before Strickland was murdered? After your husband died?"

"Visit Centurion Studios? No. Or at least I don't think so. I can't think of any reason why I should have. Not after Robert died."

"You're sure?"

"I said I don't think so. Why? Did someone say they'd seen me *there?* What difference would it make? And anyway, I'm almost positive I was never there after Robert died."

"When you've thought about it for a while, if you do remember that you were there, I'd appreciate it if you'd give me a call. For now, thank you for your cooperation."

Staver nodded to Ardis and Cooney, who escorted Vicky Jason out of the room to take her home.

Staver decided he could have flipped a coin: heads, she killed Strickland, tails, she didn't, and he'd be no worse off than he was now after her flip-flop answers to his questions.

Jim Edgell left the studio in late afternoon and drove home to Laguna in time to take a walk on the beach before the sun set. There was no one else around, and he stood for a long time at the water's edge watching a school of porpoises leaping and diving in the surf not far offshore.

When he turned to go up to the house he saw Lieutenant Staver coming across the beach toward him. He had heard that lately Staver had been suddenly popping up and surprising some of the people who had known Arthur Strickland, hoping to catch them off guard when he questioned them. Now, Edgell thought, Staver was about to try his magic *appearing* act on him.

"Mr. Edgell, how are you?" Staver asked, reaching out to shake hands.

"Fine, Lieutenant Staver. What brings you so far away from home?"

"It looked like a nice day for a ride," he answered. "And when I got around here, in your area, I thought I'd stop by, and if you were home, maybe we could talk again."

Edgell thought that was a likely story. Staver had to have been following him, but he let it ride.

"Let's go up to the house," Edgell suggested. "We can have a beer and talk."

Staver agreed that sounded like a good idea.

They climbed the steep wooden stairs from the beach to the top of the cliff and the small beach house.

Edgell opened a couple of cans of beer from the refrigerator, and they sat on the sundeck overlooking the ocean.

"The view here's as good as it is at Courtney Ware's place in Malibu," Staver said.

"The view here's a lot less expensive, too, than in Malibu," Edgell said.

"There's that." Staver nodded.

Edgell turned sideways and looked at him. "How's the investigation going? I heard you've been talking to a lot of people who knew Arthur Strickland. Somebody said you think the person who killed him was wearing a disguise, dressed like an Indian."

"We're considering that possibility, yeah." Staver took a drink of beer. "If it's true, we have to figure out who the person was."

Edgell shrugged. "I know you know it wasn't me."

"Yeah, but you see, there's always the possibility, too, that someone who wanted Strickland dead could have hired someone else to wear the disguise and kill him." Staver looked at Edgell. "You see what I mean?"

Edgell appeared surprised. "Then anyone who had any kind of grudge against Strickland is still considered a suspect?"

"You got it. And that's why I have to keep asking questions." He got up, walked across the sundeck to the railing, and looked out at the ocean as he said, "I hear Courtney Ware's going to have a baby. Don't I recall that you

252

and she were together for a while before Strickland broke you up?"

"Of course you recall that," Edgell said. "You and I talked about it at Jack King's barbecue. As far as the baby's concerned, well, that's Courtney's business."

"So it is, so it is." Staver turned from the railing. "I just thought maybe — I don't know, you might want to talk about the whole business, Strickland breaking up you and Courtney, and now the baby . . ."

Edgell shook his head. "I really don't have anything to say, Lieutenant. Except that I didn't kill him. And the baby, which, as I've said, is Courtney's business, doesn't change that fact."

"Okay," Staver said. "Thanks for the beer. Next time it's on me."

He shook hands with Edgell and left the house. He knew that Detective Murch had the house under observation from an unmarked car parked up the highway out in front. All he could hope was that his visit might have the effect of flushing Edgell out so Murch could tail him if Edgell had, in fact, hired someone to kill Strickland.

Staver hadn't expected the phone call from Halcie Harper asking him to have tea with her at Laura Harrow's house, but he'd readily accepted. Halcie Harper had a way of supplying him with startling insights in the course of the investigation.

He drove out to Laura Harrow's house; Halcie met him at the gate in front, and when he'd parked his car in the drive, led him around to the garden in back of the house.

There, at an umbrella table near the swimming pool, she honest to God served him tea.

When the tea was poured, she leaned close and whispered, "Don't look now, but Laura's watching us from that upstairs window directly behind me. You won't catch more than a glimpse, but you can take a peek up there later while we're talking."

Staver was familiar with the stories about the famous Laura Harrow being a recluse since retiring from the screen. But he still asked, "And she really doesn't allow anyone to see her?"

Halcie shook her head. "Except for her personal maid. It's sad in a way, I suppose. I've often thought that not enough credit has been paid to the great beauties of the world, considering the pleasure they've given to the rest of us, who are quite ordinary-looking."

She was speaking seriously now. "It's occurred to me that perhaps they haven't really ever been appreciated. I mean in the true sense of their contribution in adding a measure of grace to our lives. Just think of what it must be like to possess one of those beautiful faces filling an entire motion picture screen, knowing millions of eyes in the darkness of the theater are peering into that beauty as if witnessing one of the great mysteries of life. Which, indeed, they are. And what happens to the person behind that face when the beauty fades, is gone? The person must feel she's someone else altogether."

Staver glanced up at the second-floor window behind her, seeing the outline of a figure standing behind a curtain, understanding as he never would have before Laura Harrow's need for a shield from the world for the person she was now.

Halcie laughed lightly. "My goodness! I didn't mean to go on so."

Staver smiled at her. "I'm glad you did."

Halcie poured more tea. "Well, now, Lieutenant, from what I hear you've certainly been busy, subjecting almost everyone who ever knew Arthur to the — the third degree, as I think they call it."

"That's what I've been doing, all right," he agreed.

"I gather you've narrowed the suspects down

to those who were involved in making *The Amulet?* Or so it would appear from the rumors being circulated."

"That's the way I see it." He nodded. "No small thanks to you, I might add."

Halcie was delighted. "You mean because you've concluded that the killer was wearing one of the Indian costumes from the picture?"

"Since the costumes used in the production number were copies of the costumes in the movie, yes."

"And therefore it was likely that the killer had stolen a costume from wardrobe at the studio, someone connected with the movie?"

"Yes." Staver added, "The way I've reasoned it out is, the killer probably brought the disguise to the Oscars that night and would have had no trouble slipping into it, with all the activity backstage, and even slipping out of it later or perhaps leaving still wearing the disguise."

Halcie looked at him carefully. "I assume then that you checked the studio to see if any of the costumes used in the picture had disappeared before the Oscar show?"

"We checked. One of my detectives, Frank Murch, checked the studio." He sighed. "He found that the studio had already sold off the costumes to a secondhand store. We checked the store. It still had some of the costumes; some had been sold off. Their sales records were sloppy. We wound up not knowing any more than —"

He stopped in mid-sentence. "Wait a minute! Wait a minute! I should have guessed. You've found something out. You know something, don't you?"

Halcie was smiling. "Yes!"

Staver got a kick out of her enjoyment as she told him, "I wondered about the costumes, too, wondered if any were missing. When I asked, they told me the same thing, that the costumes had been sold."

She took a sip of her tea, wanting to prolong the telling of the story.

She set the cup down and said, "I knew the wardrobe mistress who worked on *The Amulet*, so I thought I'd see if I could find out anything from her. She was out of town working on location on another picture the studio's doing. She just got back today, and I talked to her. She told me that yes, before the costumes were sold, she'd gone through them and ..."

Staver said, "And one costume was missing."

Halcie nodded. "One costume and some of the ornaments, had been taken. The wardrobe mistress didn't make any great fuss about it. Frequently, after a picture is finished, someone in the crew will make off with a prop or two or a costume, to keep as a souvenir."

"That wasn't the purpose this time, I don't think," Staver said.

He looked at her and then leaned forward and kissed her on the cheek.

"Consider that," he said, "as thanks from the entire LAPD."

Jack King was sitting alone in a booth in his favorite bar, Mickey's, drinking Chivas Regal.

The TV set behind the bar was on as usual, with the sound turned down. King lit a cigar and looked without much interest at the TV screen. He watched for several minutes and saw that they were showing the film *Dial M For Murder*, which Alfred Hitchcock had directed, with Ray Milland, Grace Kelly, and Robert Cummings. He had seen the play years before on Broadway with Maurice Evans and had always thought *Dial M For Murder* was one of the three classic suspense plays ever written, along with *Witness for the Prosecution* and *Night Must Fall*.

He took a drink of his scotch and saw, with no particular surprise, Lieutenant Staver approaching the booth from the door. Still drinking from the glass, he motioned Staver to join him.

Staver slid into the seat opposite him. "How are you, Mr. King?"

King nodded. "Lieutenant." He waved a hand. "Spare me the preamble of how you just happened to be passing by, and so on. I've heard how you've been using that dialogue on everyone else you've been questioning."

Staver laughed. "Kind of corny, huh?"

Mickey came to the booth, and Staver just ordered a cup of coffee.

King took a puff of his cigar. "Your dialogue may be corny, Lieutenant, but your action is highly effective, showing up out of nowhere and asking your questions. You've had everybody spooked. Thank God we finished filming *Misplaced Affection*. Most of the people on the set couldn't take a step without turning around, expecting to see you."

"That was the idea," Staver said.

"Well, it's worked. If I deduce correctly, you're now pretty well convinced someone who worked on *The Amulet* killed Arthur."

Mickey came back with Staver's cup of coffee and left again.

Staver drank some of the coffee and told King how and why they had come to believe Strickland's killer was wearing the disguise of costume and makeup from the film, and further, that they had discovered that such items had been missing from the studio's wardrobe since before the murder. They had to suspect the killer was someone who had access to the studio and the wardrobe and props.

"I'd say it sounds like you're on the right track." King frowned. "But how did you come to count the number of performers in *The Amulet* production and then compare that number with the number of people wearing the costumes at the finale?"

"I didn't," Staver told him. "Your friend, Halcie Harper, with the help of her friend, Laura Harrow, made the discovery."

"That Halcie," King shook his head in admiration. "She's something, isn't she?"

"She sure is," Staver said.

"So." King looked at Staver. "Who do you think did it?"

Staver answered slowly. "I still don't know. But the funny thing is, I have the feeling that somewhere along the line I've already picked up the answer but I haven't yet put all the pieces together so I recognize it."

"Made the final cut, you mean," King said.

Staver looked at him blankly.

"In making films," King explained, "after you've completed all the footage — much of it shot out of sequence, some of it only brief scenes making no sense in themselves, a lot of

260

it retakes of the same scenes from which you pick the best — you look back over all of it. And you cut out shots here, splice together there, choose one scene, eliminate six, put it all together, and you have, finally, the finished picture. That's the final cut."

Staver nodded slowly. "I see," he said. "The final cut."

15

The next morning Staver drove into downtown Los Angeles from Hollywood in the early gray dawn. Most of the streets were quiet and deserted until he reached the Hollywood Freeway, where there was light traffic heading toward downtown L.A. Ahead of him the jagged skyline rose indistinct in the grayish murk, from a distance shapeless as desert peaks and canyons evolved by nature.

On the car seat beside him was his attaché case containing most of the recent paperwork collected in the Strickland investigation. He had checked through many of the papers — reports of the interrogations conducted by the other detectives and notes he had made of statements by the possible suspects he had questioned — after he had left Jack King and gone home the night before. He was reasonably sure now that somewhere in the papers was the solution to the murder. He wanted a couple of hours alone at the precinct this morning to review the whole file.

He parked behind the precinct, bought a container of coffee at the all-night coffee shop, went directly to his office, and closed the door. He emptied the papers from his attaché case onto his desk and began to arrange the interrogation reports in alphabetical order according to the last names of the subjects. As he scanned each report, he wrote the subject's name on a sheet of paper.

When he finished the list, he went down the column of names, marking an "X" to the left of each name where he believed the individual had a motive. That done, he went back down the column, marking an "X" to the right of each individual who had been at the Academy Awards.

He studied the list and the marks carefully, thinking back over all the interrogation reports he'd just read, hoping he'd find the remaining link that would positively point to the killer. The problem wasn't that it was like looking for a needle in a haystack, he thought ruefully; it was that there were too many needles in the haystack to know which was the one he was seeking.

He read the list again: every name of every-one the police knew of who had had any contact with Strickland, even names of those who couldn't possibly be the killer, such as Halcie Harper and Jack King, or who were dead, such as Richard Dald and Robert Jason. If the name of the killer was not on the list, then he had to assume it was someone who apparently was completely unknown to all those who were acquainted with Strickland. Otherwise, sometime, somewhere, during all the interrogations, the name would have surfaced.

He lit a cigarette. More than two hours had passed while he was in the office. He could hear sounds outside in the squad room as the other detectives in the Homicide Task Force arrived, although none of them would disturb him when his door was closed.

He glanced back at the list, glanced at a name on the list — and suddenly sat very still in his chair. Of course! he thought. He recalled facts that had been related to him, facts he had known, evidence he had seen but not understood, because his eye, his attention, had been cleverly diverted.

Now that he understood, he moved fast from his desk to the door, opened it, and called out to Detectives Murch, Tolbin, Tomasini, Ardis, Fried, and Cooney: "In here. On the double."

He turned back to his desk. He knew there

was no time to be lost, even though he'd still have to obtain a search warrant and arrest warrant from a judge. Meanwhile, he ordered a stakeout, sending his detectives ahead. He only hoped they weren't too late.

"See! See them there! Those two men talking on the road up there!" Courtney whispered, standing back from the window next to the front door.

"I see them, dear," Halcie said. She was standing beside Courtney at the window. "But you don't know that they're watching this house."

"I do! I do!" Courtney nodded her head impatiently. "Those other two down on the beach, too. And from the bedroom window earlier, I saw a car parked farther up the road, with two more men in the car."

Halcie didn't really know what to think. Earlier, Courtney had phoned her at Laura Harrow's house and asked her to please come out to Malibu. Courtney hadn't said on the phone what the problem was, but her voice was so pleading that Halcie had left immediately and Laura's chauffeur drove her to the beach.

She found Courtney distraught and terrified as Courtney told her there were strange men all over outside, watching the house.

Halcie did the only practical thing she could think to do. She went to the phone and called Lieutenant Staver. The operator on the switchboard told her that Staver was out of the precinct and couldn't be reached. Halcie left a message, asking that he call her, and gave the operator Courtney's number. There was no return call from the Lieutenant in the half hour Halcie had been in the house.

Halcie was on her way to the telephone to call Staver again when Courtney beckoned her back to the window, saying, "There's a car coming in the drive."

At the window again, Halcie saw Lieutenant Staver get out of the car, followed by another man. The two men who had been standing up the road now came to the front of the house. Halcie and Courtney watched from the window as the four men came to the front door and knocked.

Courtney walked stiffly to the door and opened it while Halcie waited in the background.

"Miss Ware," Staver said, his voice sounding formal and solemn, "I have a warrant authorizing me to search your premises." He held up the official document.

Courtney nodded, wordlessly.

Staver made a motion with his hand to the

other three men, and they entered the house ahead of him.

"Check everything carefully," he ordered. He closed the door behind him, and while the men spread out through the upper level of the house, he went to the den off the living room. Courtney followed behind him, and Halcie trailed after her.

Staver noticed right away that things were different in the room since the last time he was there. The desk had been cleared of the newspapers and books and magazines and pads of paper. And the rack of pipes, too, was gone.

"Lieutenant, would you please tell me what this is all about?" Courtney asked.

Staver was looking around the room. "In due time, Miss Ware. All in due time."

"Lieutenant —" Halcie started to say.

Staver turned toward her. "Miss Harper, I received your telephone message. I guess you understand now why I was unable to return your call."

"But Lieutenant —"

"Let's all just be patient for a bit," he said. He walked over to the TV set, turned on the VCR, and inserted a cassette.

He faced them again and suggested, "Why don't you both sit down?" He motioned to the sofa.

Halcie sat on the sofa and, after hesitating for a moment, Courtney sat beside her.

Detective Murch came to the door of the room. "Lieutenant," he said, "we've come up empty-handed."

Staver nodded as if the news didn't surprise him. "See if you can find anything that might give us a lead."

Murch nodded and disappeared.

Staver turned toward the sofa. "Miss Ware, what this is about is the identity of the killer of Arthur Strickland."

He turned on the TV set and then the VCR, and once again the videotape of the scene at the Academy Awards appeared on the screen.

They were all three silent until the tape reached the scene right after Strickland was stabbed and the figure in the Indian disguise could be seen from the rear. Staver pressed the Pause button and pointed to the figure.

"Arthur Strickland's killer," Staver said. He looked at Courtney. "He's your husband, Richard Dald."

"No!" Courtney shook her head.

"Yes," Staver said. "He never drowned. He just wanted everybody to think he drowned. He hid out, here, until he got his chance to kill Strickland. With your help, of course. You took the costume, the ornaments, from the studio for him to use. Afterward, he was here in this house."

"No," she said softly.

"Yes," he said. "Everything fits. The last time I was here all his things — papers, pipes — were in sight. You said you just hadn't put them away. You gave quite a performance. You're a good actress, Miss Ware."

She looked at him, saying nothing.

He stood close to her. "Everything fits. Even the baby you're going to have. His, although I guess neither of you counted on that happening."

"No," she said softly again.

This time Staver didn't answer her. He went over to the end table beside the sofa and picked up the photograph of Dald and Courtney.

"My visit the last time must have frightened him, and now he's on the run," Staver said. "But we'll get him. I'll need this photograph of him to have prints made."

He started toward the door. "Please, just stay here. I'll have more questions for you later." He went out of the room.

Detectives Murch, Tobin, and Ardis were searching the house for a possible lead to where Dald might have gone.

In the living room Ardis was flipping

269

through an address book he'd found on the telephone table.

"Find anything?" Staver asked.

"Hard to say," Ardis answered. "I think I can tell the difference between his and her handwriting in here. I'm making a copy of all the names, addresses, and phone numbers I think he made. We'll have to check them out."

"Yeah, okay."

Staver started up the stairs to the second level of the house and Tobin appeared, coming down the hall.

"I did a sweep of two of the bedrooms and the two baths, Lieutenant," Tobin said. He shook his head. "Nothing. Frank's checking out the master bedroom."

"Okay, Will. Tell you what I want you to do." Staver held out the photograph of Courtney and Dald he'd removed from the den. "Take this back to the station house. Get some prints made of Dald, get out an A.P.B. on him."

Staver crossed the upstairs hall and found Murch in the master bedroom. Murch was on his knees, looking under the king-size bed.

He stood up when Staver entered the room. "What'd the wife have to say?"

"She's all ignorance. Or so she would have us believe."

"Yeah. If she is, that puts her about even

270

with us," Murch said. "All I've been able to find is negative evidence. Empty drawers and closet space where his clothes *might* have been before he took off."

"Will says there's nothing in the other two bedrooms or the baths," Staver said. "Pete found an address book, apparently with some entries by Dald. He's making a list. I got a photo of Dald and I sent Will back to the station house to get out an A.P.B."

Murch headed for the second closet in the bedroom. "You going to take her in for questioning?" he asked back over his shoulder.

Staver was wandering around the bedroom. The decor was soft, frilly, mostly pink in color, satin in material. Definitely feminine in taste, he thought. He said, in answer to Murch's question, "I haven't decided yet. Maybe I'll let her think for a while she's fooled us into believing he really did drown. Then we'll pull her in and put the screws to her."

Murch's voice was muffled inside the closet. "Nothing in here so far. From the empty space he left, he must have had some wardrobe — Hey! — *Wait-a-minute!* I found something!"

Staver started toward the closet. Murch appeared, holding a folder in his hand. "A map! Mexico! It was on the floor, way back in the corner."

"Let's see! Let's see it!" Staver said.

Murch brought the map over and spread it out on the dresser top.

"I think this is it," he said.

There were no markings on the map. Murch asked, "What do you think, Lieutenant?"

Staver stabbed the map with a finger. "I think yes."

He looked up at Murch. "Good work, Frank. I'm going to call this in. I think we still have a good chance to catch him at the border." He started for the door and added, "And then we're going to confront 'the merry widow' with what we've found."

More to come, he thought.

Halcie had conflicting emotions after Staver left her alone with Courtney in the den. Her first impulse was to try to comfort Courtney in some way.

She asked, "Would you like tea, dear, or perhaps a drink? I'll get it."

Courtney was sitting slumped down on the sofa. "No, no, thank you. I'll be all right."

She didn't say anything else for a moment and then she turned sideways to face Halcie. "I just didn't think it would be like this, that I'd feel like this."

Halcie looked at her. "You're very unhappy, aren't you?"

"I —" Courtney wrapped her arms across her chest and nodded her head.

"Carrying a terrible secret, as you've been doing, is an intolerable burden, I'm sure," Halcie said gently. "You might have done better to have admitted the truth to Lieutenant Staver about where Richard is."

"Yes. I thought about that. I really did."

Halcie still had the impulse to try to comfort her. But then, she decided, that would be cruel. She knew what she had to say. She looked at the scene of the Oscars still on the TV set. "Isn't it strange how that videotape of Arthur's stabbing keeps coming back into our lives?"

Courtney, head lowered, said, "I guess so."

Halcie sat forward on the sofa. "Jim Edgell once told me Jack King said that because of the videotape Arthur would be returning, like Banquo's ghost in Shakespeare's *Macbeth*, to haunt us all. And he has."

When Courtney still didn't say anything, Halcie reached out with her hand and lifted Courtney's head, looking at her sympathetically.

"Richard's dead. He didn't kill Arthur," Halcie said gently. "You did. You're a better actress than even Lieutenant Staver knows."

"I – ?" There was a look of confusion on Courtney's face.

Halcie nodded. "You planned the murder, you executed it, and although for a long time nobody noticed, you went to great lengths to create the illusion that Richard was still alive. You wanted somebody to pick up the false clues you so carefully planted – that he hadn't really drowned and that he was the killer. You knew they couldn't do anything to him. It wasn't until today that your trick worked, when Lieutenant Staver himself fell for it."

Courtney was flustered. "But the videotape." She pointed to the TV set. "You yourself saw where I was standing on the stage and then saw whoever it was in the Indian disguise standing right behind Arthur when he was stabbed."

"Yes." Halcie nodded. "I know what I thought I saw. But when Lieutenant Staver replayed the tape just now, I saw I was mistaken. I saw what I hadn't seen before."

She shook her head slowly, a small smile on her face. "The other times I viewed the tape, I identified you, and where you were standing before Arthur was stabbed, by the ring on the finger of your hand. On the tape, after the stabbing, I saw the person I thought had

274

killed him, and I thought you were standing on the other side of that person. But you weren't; you *were* that person."

Courtney started to shake her head. Halcie put a hand on her arm and said, "You'd moved from where you were standing to directly behind Arthur. You stabbed him with the knife, and after the stabbing, you were standing there, in the disguise."

She patted Courtney's hand gently. "My dear, I think I can understand why you wanted revenge on Arthur for your husband's suicide. You loved Richard very much, didn't you?"

Courtney broke then. She said slowly, "Yes, I did. Very much. And Arthur — he just humiliated him so in front of everyone. I hated it that Richard killed himself. I hated Arthur for causing his death." She looked at Halcie. "But it's so strange. I never thought, at first, that I'd ever kill Arthur. Sometimes I still don't believe it."

Halcie sensed that Courtney needed to talk, and remained silent while Courtney tried to explain all that happened to her between the time of Richard's suicide and now.

At first, she reminded Halcie, right after Richard drowned himself, she had had a nervous collapse, she was in a clinic in the desert and was given drugs. Then, when she was recovered, Jim Edgell tried to help her and she stayed with him in Laguna. "Jim was so sweet, so caring. I really regret that I had to hurt him, but I knew I had to put him out of my life once I'd decided what I was going to do. So I came back here, away from Jim."

Her voice was tired as she told Halcie how she had come back to the house in Malibu and was confronted with all of Richard's belongings — clothes, books, papers, his pipe collection. His presence in the house was very strong, she said. And then she began to think what it would be like if he hadn't drowned, but had only pretended, and had planned his revenge on Strickland. She began to imagine how he would go about taking revenge, and she found herself plotting out exactly when and where and how he would kill Strickland.

"Meanwhile, every day," she said, "I was working on the set and hating Arthur. I saw he was cruel and arrogant, misusing his power."

She had concluded that Richard would have decided that the Academy Awards, if Strickland won an Oscar, would be the right place, and the right time, to kill him — the ultimate humiliation.

"The rest was easy to plot," Courtney said. "I did it exactly the way you figured. When they first announced the Oscar nominees, they said there would be a production number set to the music of *The Amulet* and using costumes copied from the picture. So I managed to remove one of the costumes and some ornaments from the studio before they were sold off. Of course, there was no way I could have known in advance they'd be videotaping everything directly afterward. It was just luck that saved me for a while because you spotted the ring I was wearing."

She glanced at the TV set. "You know, if Arthur and I hadn't won an Oscar, he'd never have been killed then and there. We both had to be on the stage for the finale. And you know something else?" She paused.

"What's that?" Halcie asked.

"I still could never have done it," Courtney said, "if I hadn't pretended all the time it was happening that I was Richard. You know how it is when you're playing a role sometimes, you try to lose your sense of yourself and become the character? I was Richard, in that disguise, when I stabbed Arthur. Then I slipped away to one of the dressing rooms, where I'd put on the costume between the time I won the Oscar and the finale, and changed back into my gown, and returned to the stage. I was no longer Richard. Nobody noticed."

"You got the idea of making it look as if

Richard hadn't drowned from the plot of *The Amulet,* didn't you? Where the boyfriend didn't drown, and comes back?"

"Yes," Courtney said. "I did think of that at first when Richard drowned, and all the rest of it followed when I started to plan what I was going to do."

"And the baby you said you were expecting?" Halcie asked.

Courtney shook her head. "I'm not pregnant. I wish I were. I made that up, too, hoping someone would see it as more proof that Richard was still alive, the way Lieutenant Staver did today. I was going to continue to add padding to my clothing as time went on. Then, eventually, of course, if my plan worked, I would go into seclusion before I announced I'd had a miscarriage. You see," she added fiercely, "I wanted the whole world to think Richard had been clever enough to have killed Arthur and gotten away with it!"

"And that's almost the way it would have happened." It was Lieutenant Staver, standing in the open doorway.

Neither woman had noticed him there. Halcie looked up at him, distressed, but Courtney was calm as she asked, "You heard, Lieutenant?"

"Enough." He didn't look particularly happy.

278

"I'm glad, really," Courtney said.

Now it was she who patted Halcie's hand. "It would have been too great a burden for Halcie to be the only one to know, besides me. I wouldn't have wanted that."

She leaned over and kissed Halcie on the cheek. "The truth is, it was too great a burden for me." She turned to Staver. "I imagine you want me to go with you."

"Yes," he said, "please."

He went over to Halcie for a moment. "You did it. You discovered what we've been looking for all along. Remember? Where the truth lies."

"What I discovered in the process," Halcie said, "is what we know is often the fact but sometimes forget."

"And what's that?"

"That we can be fooled by what we think is certain to be true. I was certain that Courtney, because of where she was standing, couldn't have killed Arthur. And I was certain that whoever was standing behind Arthur had killed him. What I had forgotten, until I finally caught it on the tape today, was that, more often than not, where the truth lies is somewhere in between."

Staver started away and then turned back. "Tell me something: How in the world did you solve this case?"

Halcie had a twinkle in her eye when she answered. "It was easy. Don't you remember those times I played Miss Marple in films? I learned how to spot a red herring — as they call it — when I see one."

The heat seemed trapped in the thick yellowish smog enveloping L.A., so there was no escaping it outdoors on the summer day Halcie returned to Centurion Studios to pose for a series of still photographs before she left for New York. The photographs would be sent out to the media by Eddie McCoy, along with a press release, when *Misplaced Affection* opened in movie theaters across the country later in the year.

This was the first time Halcie had been back at the studio since they'd finished shooting *Misplaced Affection,* since before Courtney had been arrested and released on bail pending her trial. Halcie had heard that Jim Edgell was again constantly with Courtney, to comfort her and give her encouragement.

One night during that time Lieutenant Staver and Zoe had taken Halcie to dinner. Halcie had wondered what would happen to Courtney, and Staver emphasized that solving the Strickland case was the most important thing. He said that once the story of the murder was told, it was up to the people — as he phrased it — to decide what should happen to Courtney.

On this day, after the photography session ended, Halcie went looking for Jack King, who had told her earlier on the phone that he would be working in one of the studio editing rooms.

"Halcie!" King greeted her, kissing her on both cheeks. She had found him in a room crowded with several film-editing machines, with tables piled high with cans of film, and with reels of film stacked one on top of the other next to the machines. Patricia Banks, film editor on *Misplaced Affection,* was with him.

"You're sure I'm not interrupting?" Halcie asked.

"Your timing is, as always, perfect," he assured her, waving her to a chair. "We need a break."

Patricia, after shaking hands with Halcie, told King she was going to the commissary for coffee and a cigarette, and left.

King pulled a chair up close to Halcie. "So you're really going to leave us?"

She nodded. "It's back to the Big Apple tomorrow."

"I don't think you'll ever forget working on this film," King said.

"No, no, I don't think so." She looked at the

281

stacks of film. "How's the picture turning out?"

"Actually," he said with a nod, "the final cut's done. All we're doing now is sifting through the bits and pieces left over. I thought I might find one closing shot that was exactly right for the ending."

"You mean following the final scene where the three women say good-bye at the airport?"

"A closing image to leave with our audience," he said.

He stood up and went to one of the editing machines, motioning for Halcie to follow him. "I just put this footage on to take a look at. They're protection shots I made of close-ups of Zoe's face and Courtney's and yours. Let's watch."

He turned on the machine. Halcie saw Zoe's face as King said, "Remember, the audience has seen that she was jilted at the altar. Now I cut to Courtney's face — see, she lost a husband. And now I cut to your face — see, you were dumped in a divorce."

He stopped the film. Halcie's face was still on the screen.

"You see it?" he asked. "The faces of three women who have experienced life at different stages, and you can see from their faces that they've not only endured but prevailed. Three faces that could be one woman, or all women."

Halcie kissed him. "Oh, Jack, I like it."

King hugged her. He was pleased. He turned off the editing machine. Halcie's face disappeared from the screen. He said:

"That's our fade-out."

THORNDIKE PRESS HOPES you have enjoyed this Large Print book. All our Large Print titles are designed for the easiest reading, and all our books are made to last. Other Thorndike Press Large Print books are available at your library, through selected bookstores, or directly from the publisher. For more information about current and upcoming titles, please call us, toll free, at 1-800-223-6121, or mail your name and address to:

THORNDIKE PRESS
P. O. BOX 159
THORNDIKE, MAINE 04986

There is no obligation, of course.